Johnny's Story

Johnny's Story

Having the Gift of Enough

Andy Smith

TKR Publishing
Nashville, TN

Cover by Berta Martinez

Contents

JOHNNY'S STORY

HAVING THE GIFT OF ENOUGH

by Andy Smith

Dedication

I dedicate this book to
The Jones
Because everyone is trying To keep up with The Jones
So maybe if they learn To have ENOUGH
The rest of us could finally Relax!

Disclaimer

As a writer, it's always a good feeling when you type the words, 'The End'. Your story has taken you – and hopefully readers to come – on a journey of adventure that has brought us to those magical words of conclusion. Your adventure has come to an end and now, as a writer, it's merely a matter of going over your work to edit, tighten up and rewrite your story until you are completely satisfied that it is worthy to share with your fan base of loyal readers. I know it sounds like a lot of effort for eleven people, but a writer never looks at the numbers. I approach every new creation with an attitude that my readers – no matter the number – deserve nothing less than my best effort.

Johnny's Story was fun to write. It's funny, when I was a budding writer, I gave very little thought of writing fiction. I was a non-fiction writer who loved taking real life situations and giving them the light-hearted humorous voice they needed to entertain. I didn't read a novel until I was in my sixties. I appreciated fantasies and stories of make believe in theaters, but I never thought of that style of writing to be on my menu.

Then I had a dream that inspired my last book, *My First Seven Days in Heaven and More*. I had so much fun writing that book, and it was a completely different experience as a writer than anything else I had written. I never knew exactly where I was going with my story, but it was fiction and I didn't have to worry about making it 'real' as you do non-fiction so I just sat back and let the story take me wherever it wanted to go.

What a fun ride writing fiction.

So of course, when I had a dream that inspired the idea for *Johnny's Story*, I didn't hesitate. I got my fingers cranked up and ready for a new adventure. Sure enough, this new fiction was even better than the last. I had no idea where the story was headed, but I trusted my fingers and with each chapter I started, the ideas would come that took a turn here and another turn there until I typed 'The End' and found my story of *Having The Gift Of Enough* to be a creative masterpiece.

I now truly look forward to going to bed every night, not because I'm tired but because I can't wait for another crazy dream to inspire the ideas for my next story. Who knew writing fiction could be so much fun?! Well, probably most people. It took me well over sixty years on this planet to figure out that I might be better off writing fiction instead of non-fiction, but who's counting, right? At least I figured it out!

So now I'm done. I have started another story and have

reached the glorious moment of typing 'The End'. Time for me to step away from the desk, go make myself a drink and celebrate that I have finished another great story that most of the people on this planet will never read!

As I get to my kitchen and turn on the light, I am SHOCKED to find a young man sitting out in my recliner chair.

"Who the hell are you and what are you doing in my home!" I say in absolute fear.

"It's me, Chris. Your guardian angel. Remember me from *My First Seven Days in Heaven*?" He says as if it was a silly question.

As I take a closer look, he does resemble the vision of my guardian angel I had when I was writing *7Days*, but for crying out loud, that was fiction and this guy is now literally sitting in my living room as if he is a welcomed guest, which he is NOT!

"What are you doing here?"

"We need to talk. God is not very happy with you." he says somewhat remorseful.

I stare at him for a brief moment as I realize I need to make my drink a double, so I get busy with my creation as I formulate my response.

"God is not happy with ME? I'm a retired old man with little going on outside of my grandkids. I watch the evening news, pal, and I'm pretty sure there is plenty going on all over this planet to give God concerns. I think you're a tad overreaching to think that God would be unhappy about me when he really should be pissed off at so many others." I say as I finish making my drink.

"That's the point, buddy boy. God chose you to deliver his message and here you are publishing these stories as fiction!"

"WHAT!?! You're crazy! I just made this stuff up." I say with a strong dose of firmness.

"Wrong! They were created from dreams you had, correct?" Chris says with that annoying smile. What is it about angels and their constant smug smiles?

"Exactly. They were created from DREAMS, which is fiction, not non-fiction!"

"Wrong again. Can you imagine how different the world would be if Joseph looked at his dreams as fiction? There are so many examples of history changing course that had it's very beginnings with a dream. God uses dreams often to get his message out."

"Yea, well Joseph lived in a different world than I do. They didn't read books or go to movies and stuff like that. They paid more attention to their dreams back then. If God wants someone to take a dream in today's world and make it non-fiction, he's got to make it very clear, that's for sure."

Chris just smiles that smile in pause before responding.

"That's why I'm here, buddy boy. God wants me to make it perfectly clear that the stories you are writing are absolutely, positively non-fiction and he wishes you would stop publishing then as fiction, okay?!"

"No it's not okay, BUDDY BOY! To be non-fiction, the story has to have a factual foundation created from reality, not just a cool idea from a dream." I say with a strong dose of annoyance at his smug smiles and reference to me as 'Buddy Boy'.

It occurs to me that these feelings I am having are the same I had when I was writing *7Days* and having conversations with Chris in that story, which makes me realize that this conversation is likely nothing more than falling asleep at my desk and having yet another bazar dream. This makes my follow up response one that will bring this dreamy conversation to an end so I can wake up and go about my editing.

"Besides, if God really wants to get his message out, why wouldn't he pick Mitch Albom or someone like that who actually has a following? Ya gotta admit that picking me to get his message out is a pretty lame choice, and I'm thinking God is smarter than that." I say with a tone of my own smugness.

"Well Andy, I learned a long time ago not to question the people God chooses to bring his message. John the Baptist wasn't exactly a Boy Scout, ya know. And the twelve disciples Jesus chose to follow him were not exactly your prim 'n proper fellas that people wanted to listen to. I'd be happy to go over all the people in history that God has chosen to present his message if you'd like, but I think you already know that God chooses people because of their heart, not their resume." he says with the impact of a punch in the gut.

I pause in consideration of what he is saying, which of course always makes sense.

"Chris, I hear what you're saying, but there is no way I can publish these books as nonfiction. They have rules in publishing, you know. If I publish these as non-fiction, I'll have to be able to prove that the stories are based on factual ideas, not dreams."

Chris smiles, "And if you stood firm on the truth, they would have to prove that it is fiction, right?"

I wasn't ready for that reply.

"But how do I know the truth? This may be nothing more than another dream I'm having?"

"If you wake up at your desk, or in your bed, fair enough. But you might want to fix yourself another drink because God can certainly out last you. I promise you that after I leave, God will keep you awake as long as it takes to get you to understand this conversation."

Another good point. Another punch in the gut.

"How about a compromise. I'll write a disclaimer to explain that I have to publish these stories as fiction and that the reader should seriously consider that these stories should be nonfiction, but proving the reality of the hereafter is not an easy thing to do?"

Chris smiles, "Well if that's the best you can do, we'll have to work with it. I just came to let you know God wasn't very happy about publishing these stories as fiction."

As we stare at each other, it dawns on me.

"Wait a minute, Chris. So you're saying that everything I wrote in *7Days* and *Johnny's Story* is actually true?"

Chris smiles, "You said it before how every time you

started a new chapter, you had no idea what direction you were heading, right? That happens all the time when God is working with people to get his message out. You think you have it tough with publishers, you should have heard the conversation Joseph had in trying to explain to Mary how they needed to get up and head for Egypt right after she gave birth to Jesus. That Joseph was a man of faith, that's for sure."

With that, Chris disappears from my living room, leaving me to choose between the fiction and non-fiction of life.

So there you have it, my loyal readers. It's up to you to decide fiction or non-fiction on these stories of mine. But be careful. It took me two weeks of no sleep before I finally sat down to write this disclaimer.

The choice is yours.

I'm going to bed!

The author

IF YOU ALWAYS

PRAY FOR MORE

YOU'LL NEVER HAVE

ENOUGH

IF YOU ALWAYS

PRAY FOR ENOUGH

YOU'LL NEVER NEED

MORE

PART I

Life

At The

Pub

1

___

The Santa

Johnny is quietly resting on his usual stool at his local neighborhood Pub. He didn't come to the Pub every night. Two or three times a week, maybe four, and seldom the same days. He always likes to sit at the end of the bar right next to the servers station so he can casually visit with the coming and going servers of the night.

Everyone knows Johnny. A retired man who has been alone for the past eight years after his wife, Beth, passed away. A simple man. Not loud, but not unapproachable. Johnny was not one to start a conversation, but was always willing to engage with those who did. There was no topic off limits when you spoke with Johnny, which made him a regular at the Pub you didn't mind grabbing the seat next to when you walked in. A nice guy. Never wanting the spotlight. Always interested in your world and how you looked at the events of the day. A good listener.

For the past month or so, the seat next to Johnny could

be occupied by Joe. Joe was more of a mysterious man than Johnny. Nobody knew what he did or where he lived. He'd come into the Pub now and then and always welcomed the empty seat next to Johnny. He enjoyed starting a conversation, but he always kept it about world events and seldom talked about himself. Claims to be a writer, but never wants to carry the conversation down that road. Not a loud man. A nice guy. Carried himself well. Wore nice clothes- clearly this was a man with good taste.

Most of the regulars thought Joe probably lived near the city. Probably one of those nice condos with a killer view. Every time he was asked what brought him out this way, he'd always just say research.

Joe just seemed like the kind of guy who could fit into any group, any conversation. The regulars at the Pub looked at him more as another regular than an intruder. You felt comfortable around Joe and he never came across as better than you, though his appearance and conversation suggested he likely was.

Whatever research Joe was doing, he seemed more than happy to end up at the Pub. He especially enjoyed it when he could find Johnny sitting at the end of the bar. In fact, if there was someone else sitting next to Johnny when Joe walked in, there would be an automatic shift in seats to make room for Joe next to Johnny. It was always a good night when Joe and Johnny occupied the end of the bar.

On this particular evening, the conversation centered around a baseball player who was complaining that he was only getting paid ten million dollars a year when lesser players were getting over fifteen million. That was always a fun conversation at a watering hole as the hard working, blue collar folks loved bashing those who have so much more. But it also lends itself to some great conversations of what each patron would do if they had a mere ten million dollars a year to live on.

Johnny never jumped into these conversations. He mostly enjoyed listening to the others and only added a comment now and then. Joe was the same. Enjoyed listening to everyone else, only throwing out questions from time to time of a different perspective to stir things up. But eventually, the conversation would make it's way to the end of the bar.

"What do you think about it Johnny?" a regular would ask.

"Well, if I buy a ticket to go to a ball game, I'm going to see the third baseman play, not to watch the owner sitting up in his luxury box. If the player wants some of the owners money, I don't have a problem with that. Haven't seen too many owners going broke, have you?"

Everyone gets a good laugh whenever Johnny speaks.

"But isn't it wrong to be so greedy when there are so many who struggle?" asks one of the servers.

Johnny softly responds, "Greed is a problem at every level, not just the wealthy. Everyone wants more. Nobody has enough. The key to a happy life is to learn to be satisfied with enough."

Johnny has the ability to put a bow on the conversation.

He always seems to have the right words, the right perspective that puts a conversation to bed.

As most of the patrons move onto a new topic or into their own private conversations, Joe turns to Johnny with a confident smile, "You are a wise man, Johnny, but do you think there are people who actually have enough?"

"I'd say so. I think I have enough and have no desire to pursue more than I have."

"So you're say'n that if you won a ten million dollar lottery, you wouldn't be excited?"

"Of course I'd be excited. I've never played the lottery and have no idea how it works, so if I won ten million dollars, it'd be the biggest story since Jesus being born of a virgin."

Joe laughs, "I suppose that would be something. Well I've got enough to buy you a drink, so let me get you one."

Johnny smiles, "I appreciate that. One more and then I have to go."

"Where do you go from here, Johnny?"

"I take the bus over to the cemetery to visit Beth – my wife – It's always a nice visit when I can get there right at sunset."

"How long has she been gone?" Joe asks

"Been eight years on Christmas day."

"Your wife died on Christmas day? Man that had to be rough." says Joe as another round of drinks is delivered.

"Beth loved the holidays. She'd been sick for a bit so it wasn't much of a surprise when she left. In many ways, I think it's fitting that she stopped suffering on her favorite day of the year."

"She must have been a special lady."

Johnny looks distant with a subtle smile, "Indeed she was. Married to me for 54 years and not once caused me a moments grief. I was a lucky man."

Joe takes a moment to let the mood settle before continuing, "Is it hard for you when the holidays come around?"

Johnny hesitates in thought, but responds, "No, not really. I had a good life with Beth. No regrets at all. She no longer suffers and that gives me comfort. Besides, I have a standing order to play Santa Clause every year at the mall outside of town. I enjoy talking to the kids."

Joe laughs, "You're Santa Clause?!"

"I enjoy it. Keeps my mind on the holidays and keeps me from pouting about Beth not being here. She really did Christmas big."

Joe pauses for another sip, "I bet you're a great Santa. So if Santa could give these kids anything, what would you give them."

Johnny looks to Joe with confidence, "Enough."

Joe is a bit surprised with Johnny's answer, "Enough?"

"Sure, everybody wants more. More toys, more money, more titles and recognition. So every Christmas I try to tell the kids that happiness comes to those who understand the magic of having enough."

Joe thinks about it, then continues, "That's a nice thought, Johnny, but do they buy it?"

"The children do for the most part but the parents, not so

much. They always seem so frazzled in thinking they have to buy more this year than they did last year. It's never enough for parents."

"I guess most parents feel they are bad parents if they don't have a lot of boxes under the tree, right."

"If they keep buying more toys, the kids only learn to just want more. But if you read them a story, give them a hug and tell them how much you love them every night, the kids will never want, they'll always have enough."

Johnny takes a final splash from his drink and gets up to leave, " Well Joe, the sunset doesn't wait for me, so I better move on."

Joe pats his friend on the back, "You're a good man, Johnny. And a good Santa. I appreciate my time spent on this seat."

As Johnny leaves the Pub, Joe orders one more drink and reflects on the conversation they just had.

One of the servers comes to the station to order a glass of Merlo and Pinot Grigio for table 15.

Joe breaks from his thoughts and engages with her, "Tell me young lady, If Santa could give you anything, what would you ask for?"

The girl smiles, "Really?"

"Sure. If Santa could give you anything in the world, what would you ask for?"

The girl shakes her head, but considers the question, "Well I'd probably ask for a dependable car so I can get to school and work on time."

Joe smiles, "Anything in the world, and you'd ask for a car?"

As the girl balances her drinks, she responds, "Yeah. If I have a mansion or travel the world, I want it to be on my dime, not some fat guy who wears red suits and hangs out with reindeers."

As she heads to table 15, Joe laughs, then asks Sue the bartender, who is cleaning off Johnny's spot, what the servers name is.

Sue smiles, "That's Kim, she's a rather independent girl."

"She is that." confirms Joe as he gets up to leave, "She is that."

2

The Debate

Another early evening at the Pub with Johnny in his usual spot at the end of the bar. It's been a rainy day for the third day in a row, so everyone seems to be talking about the weather.

As Johnny quietly sits sipping his usual, one of the servers comes to the station to order another round of beers for the boys at table 10. While she's waiting on the beers, she takes advantage of the moment to visit with Johnny. "You think it's ever going to stop raining, Johnny?"

"Well I haven't seen any of my neighbors building an ark yet, so I'm guessing it will stop eventually"

The server laughs as she balances the beers and heads over towards table 10. As she does, she greets Joe who has just entered the Pub and is shedding his rain gear.

"How's it going, Joe? Wet enough for you out there?"

Joe smiles, "Indeed."

Joe makes his way over to the seat next to Johnny and after the usual segue, jumps into the conversation of the evening.

"Somebody is going to have to explain to me that when the weatherman says there is a 60% chance of rain today, what should we expect if it's 100% chance of rain?"

Everyone smiles in agreement as Joe orders his drink from Sue.

"You know it's all about that global warming stuff they're talking about" says one of the servers, always happy to jump in and stir the conversation. You always make better tips when the conversations start to heat up.

"Here we go," says Eric, one of the Pub regulars who always stands firmly on the political right, " Another discussion from the liberal left pouting about how human progress and ingenuity is killing our precious planet."

"Well you can't argue with all the scientists who clearly agree that human progress and greed is killing our planet." says another regular, MaryJo.

Eric laughs, "ALL the scientists? I promise you, girl, for every 'study' you give me from all these scientists who know everything, I can show you a study from other scientists – that apparently don't exist in your world – that makes a pretty good argument that the planet goes through cycles and has been since the beginning of time, and we are simply going through one of those adjustments that most planets in the universe goes through."

"It's attitudes like yours that convinces me that the real

scientists are right. People are so selfish and greedy that they refuse to be sensitive to the health of our planet."

Eric laughs out loud again, "You liberals are so sensitive. You pout and cry about global warming when you see the fires out in California, and next year you'll be out there taking beautiful pictures of the very same landscape that is now bouncing back with a vibrant renewal of life as those same scientists explain how our planet is so strong in it's ability to heal and renew itself. No matter what natural disaster we are watching today, I guarantee you that next year we'll be watching reports on how well the planet has bounced back and become even stronger."

MaryJo shakes her head in disgust, "Well we'll see what you think when you come in here with an oxygen tank in tow because you can't breath."

Eric smiles, "You liberals. You see the planet as this precious, delicate ball that we need to coddle and protect without realizing that this planet has been adjusting to all the climate changes, natural disasters and inter-galactic events of space for millions of years and will continue to do so regardless of what we mere humans try to do. You guys are always whining about being lactose intolerant, you can't eat this salad because your tummy is sensitive to walnuts, you can't go to the beach because your skin is extra sensitive to the direct sunlight. I don't know how you liberals sleep at night. The truth is that God gave us a wonderful planet that is always evolving and adjusting to the cycles of life, and he gave us wonderful bodies that can – and will always- adjust to the many complex evolutions of our environment. You guys just have no faith."

MaryJo shakes her head again, "You're an idiot" to Eric. "Sue, can I get another drink here?" she says to the bartender.

Eric laughs, "Well the good news, MaryJo, is that you are not alcohol intolerant and neither am I." he turns to Sue behind the bar, "Miss Sue, could you get me another drink as well, and put MaryJo's drink on my tab, would you. I'm pretty sure my selfish greed can afford to buy my friend a drink."

MaryJo shakes her head and holds up her glass in salute to Eric, who does likewise, as the rest of the Pub merrily moves on to other conversations as this one has come to an impasse. Neighborhood bar rules are always understood that when a conversation gets to ordering another round, that conversation is over and it's time to move on.

Joe and Johnny have been quietly enjoying the debate, and as Joe orders another drink as well, he turns to Johnny, "I always love those debates about the world coming to an end, don't you Johnny?"

"Well they both make good arguments, but like most issues, the real answer usually lies somewhere in-between the two." says Johnny.

"What do you think, Johnny? You think the world is coming to and end?"

Johnny looks over to Joe with a confident smile, "Well I think mine is. I just celebrated my 84th last week. I'm guessing I don't have too many more laps around the Sun."

Joe smiles, "You know, I've often felt the problem with America is that they put the government in those big, cold marble buildings in DC. They'd probably get a lot more accomplished if they instead put three nice neighborhood Pubs around there. The congress could hang out in one, the senate another, and the White House the third. They can bar hop from one to the other until they can find that middle ground that you and most Americans hang out in, and then claim it as the law of the land. There's just nothing better than a glass of wine to break down the politically correct conversation and find the fertile common ground of truth."

Johnny smiles in agreement, "Well if you run for President on that platform, I'll certainly vote for you."

Joe laughs, "I assure you Johnny, I wouldn't last very long in the capital. I'm far too honest."

Johnny lays down his cash and gets up to leave, "Well that's the rub, Joseph. When honesty is a liability in governing, then you no longer have a government for the people, do you?"

"You are correct, Johnny boy. I suppose you are indeed, correct."

As Johnny pops his umbrella to exit into the watery muck of the evening, Joe orders another drink. As he waits for his drink, Kim comes to the servers station to order another round for the big gathering at table 7. They are a loud group that appears to be celebrating something.

"Sounds like your table is having a good time tonight, Kim."

"Yeah. The older guy is retiring, so they are all sending him off. He's a free man from now on." says Kim with a hint of jealousy.

"So Kim, do you think the world is coming to an end?"

"I hope not. People who talk about the doomsday world are people who have given up. I have faith in life and am excited to tackle whatever comes my way. I hope I'm around for my retirement party so I can look back and see all that I've accomplished."

As Kim carefully situates her many drinks on her tray, Joe starts to get up to leave.

"Did Santa get you that car yet?"

Kim laughs, "Ha! No, but he's a guy whose been riding around forever in an old sleigh with a bunch of Reindeers pulling him. I'm not sure I'd want him picking out a car for me."

"What kind of car would you want?"

As she heads for table 7, she replies, "Something that gets me from point A to point B on time!"

Joe shakes his head in appreciation as he signs his bill and heads out.

3

———

The Tip

As the Fall season settles into the sleepy town, Joe settles into the seat next to Johnny. He notices the Santa hat sticking out of his vest pocket, which seems like the perfect starting point for this evening's conversation.

"Don't tell me they're making you play Santa before Thanksgiving?" he says with a tone of despair.

Johnny laughs, "No, I just went by to pick up my suit and listen to the young marketing gurus tell me what's new at the stores and what toys I need to push."

MaryJo shakes her head, "Marketing – a necessary evil that gets way too much credit for doing what basically amounts to nothing more than annoying people into buying things they don't need."

Johnny tosses the comment aside, "Guess they gotta pay their rent too. I don't listen much to their sales pitch, though. I get paid to listen to the kids, not the marketing folks."

Joe likes the response, "So when do you start ho, ho, hoing?"

"Thanksgiving Day. Have to be there around noon."

"It's a shame you have to go in on Thanksgiving Day." says Eric.

"Oh I don't mind, really. Beth was a great cook – I'm not. They put out a nice spread for all the workers. It's really not a bad day to go in really."

Joe takes a sip of his drink in thought, "Tell me, Johnny, what's the strangest thing a kid has asked you for?"

Johnny pauses and takes a sip from his drink as he considers the question.

"Well I suppose the strangest thing was a young boy who asked me for a watermelon."

Everybody laughs.

"A kid asked you for a watermelon?" says Eric in disbelief.

"Oh bless that poor child's heart." says MaryJo.

"How do you know he's poor? Maybe he just likes watermelon." says Eric always happy to jump on MaryJo's sensitive nature.

"Oh hush, " says MaryJo, "Don't try to pretend that you care."

Eric laughs, "I'm just saying – I'd love a watermelon for Christmas, but they're not in season. Hard to find a good watermelon at Christmas."

MaryJo orders another drink, "But you sure can find a lot of coal this time of year, right Eric?"

Eric laughs, "I have the best bar-b-ques every Summer.

You should plan to come by some time." then he turns to Johnny, "So what did you tell the young lad, Johnny?"

"I asked him why he wanted a watermelon and he said some of the kids talk about how much they love watermelon, and he's never had one."

MaryJo sighs, "How sweet. I hope he gets one."

Johnny looks to MaryJo, "He did. I know the family. They struggle a lot. I had a kid drop it off the next morning with a gift card for the grocery store"

"Why aren't you the best Santa ever!" says MaryJo, "Are most of the kids you talk to struggling?"

"For the most part. That part of town has a lot of hard working families that are just trying to get up to zero. Most of the kids don't ask for much because they know they won't get it. I have to really work the Santa thing in order to keep the magic of Christmas alive."

MaryJo perks up with excitement, "I think we should all help Santa keep the spirit of Christmas for these kids, what do you say?"

Eric doesn't hesitate, "I'm in."

MaryJo looks at him as if to be waiting on a punch line.

Eric responds confused, "What, you think only the liberals have a heart? I happen to know a guy who lives out that way. Hard working, good guy, loves his kids, but hates Christmas. He can't even afford a Christmas tree this year. He barely makes enough to pay his bills."

"That's it!" says MaryJo, so excited she can barely keep up with the words flying out of her mouth, "We're going to help this man's family out. Everybody lay some cash on the bar. Eric's going to buy a Christmas tree for them, " she pauses and looks to Eric, "Do you know where he lives?"

"Well not really, but I'm sure it's not hard to find out."

MaryJo doesn't stop, "Good. You buy the tree and deliver it to his home without his family knowing where it came from."

Eric jumps in, to cool things down, "Hold on lefty!,' (Eric loves to call MaryJoy lefty due to her political attributes) "I do know that he owns a pit bull who could be less than cordial when strangers come by. That's a scary part of town, ya know."

MaryJoy pauses in thought, "I guess if I was a Pit Bull, I'd love to take a chunk out of your leg too. Well figure something out. Just don't let him know where it came from. This is going to be a great Christmas for this family." MaryJo is basking in the warmth of the conversation.

As the conversation continues and people approach the bar to lay down their money, Joe turns to Johnny again.

"You know, I can help you out if you come across any special needs for the kids this year. Just get their names and whatever info you can gather without being too obvious, and I'll make sure those kids get what they need."

Johnny smiles, "You're jealous of me being Santa Clause, right?"

Joe laughs, "Indeed. But I wouldn't mind being a Santa's helper. You just let me know those families that are really struggling and find out what would be enough for them to have a nice Christmas."

Johnny shakes his head, "I don't know, Joe, there's a lot of families like Eric's friend over that way. You might be sorry you asked."

Joe smiles, "I trust you Johnny. You know the families over there. You know the ones who always want more and those who only want enough. You tell me about those who simply want enough, and I'll work it out."

Johnny looks at Joe, "Just want enough? Well that narrows the field down somewhat, but I know there are some good families like Eric's friend."

"Great," says Joe as he turns his attention to a conversation at the servers station.

Sue and Kim have been talking while Sue loads up Kims tray with waters and drinks. She seems a bit down today. Not her usual engaging personality.

"The car repairs cost almost $200 dollars and I have to have my car. But now I'm told if I don't pay $142 dollars tomorrow, my lights go out. It only takes one thing to throw everything else off. So I'm going to pretty much work through the holidays. I need to get out of this financial pit a whole lot more than taking time off for family, that's for sure."

"That sucks," says Kim as she prepares to head to table 12, "And people don't tip as well during the holidays. They're spending all their money on more gifts."

As Kim heads towards table 12 and Sue gets another round for Eric, MaryJo takes over the conversation.

"So Eric, do you think you have enough for a tree?"

"I think I have enough for a forest." he says as he looks at the mound of money in front of him. "I don't think this guy has that big a house."

"Just buy a nice tree and put the rest of the money in an envelope that says 'Have a great Christmas' Keep it anonymous and don't put the envelope down where the pit bull can get to it, put it up high. But be careful that it's not seen by people walking by."

Eric interrupts MaryJo, "Okay, okay, okay! I got it, Lefty. I know a kid who would do it for me. We'll get it done."

As Eric and MaryJo start counting out the money, Joe turns to Johnny.

"Let me buy Santas drinks tonight, Johnny" as he hands Sue his credit card, indicating it wasn't a point of discussion.

"Thanks, Joe. So what are you doing for Thanksgiving?"

Joe smiles, "Research. I'm always doing research."

"Must be a pretty good story you're writing. Or a pretty difficult one. You do a lot of research."

"Research is what life is all about, Johnny. The more you research, the more your story grows."

As they get up to head for the door, Johnny notices the bill on the bar. As they reach the door, Johnny speaks up.

"$142 tip is pretty good for a couple of drinks, don't you think?"

Joe smiles at Johnny, "It was enough."

Johnny turns back and sees Sue looking at the receipt with her hand over her mouth and tears welling up in her eyes.

"Enough Indeed." he smiles.

4

The Payback

As the Thanksgiving holiday fades, the Pub scene settles into a normal holiday routine of the hustle and bustle of holiday shoppers popping in for a drink and being tight with the tips as expected by all servers. Servers who work the holidays understand that most shoppers don't tip well, but there are always a few customers whose spirit of generosity serves well to balance out the evenings. The holidays are a lot busier, but you consider yourself lucky to go home with about the same tips of any other time of the year. That's just the way it is.

MaryJo makes her way into the bar and seems excited to see Eric with an empty seat next to him. As she removes her coat, hat and scarf and settles in, she is quick to cut out the usual pleasantries and jumps right into the main entre for tonight's conversation.

"So Eric, tell me how the Christmas tree gift went for your friend."

Eric, always happy to take a jab at lefty, "Well hello lefty,

I'm fine, thank you. How was your Thanksgiving?" he says with sarcasm dripping from every word.

MaryJo blows him off of course, "HaHaHa. We can get to that later. I've been dying to find out how your friends tree gift worked out." as Sue delivers her drink she didn't ask for because that's what makes a regular a regular.

Eric understands he needs to just move with the conversation without any further commentary. "It went well. No problems at all. "

MaryJo doesn't let Eric finish, "Was there any problems with the dog?"

Eric smiles, "Actually the kid I had deliver it said that was one of the nicest dogs he's ever met. He only feared being licked to death."

MaryJo laughs out loud with several of the other regulars joining in. "Isn't that funny. Tell people you have a pit bull and everyone assumes you have a monster. I have a friend who owns one and the only problem I have is getting bruises on my legs because she jumps up to love on me so much. Those dogs are solid, that's for sure. So have you seen your friend? Does he seem really upbeat and positive? Tell me everything."

Eric puts down his drink, "Hold on there, lefty. I said I knew him, I didn't say we were joined at the hip. He works in maintenance at my company. I've talked to him a few times "

"Ah isn't that sweet. You actually talk to the lesser people" she counters with her own sarcasm.

Eric shakes his head and smiles, "Yes, we righties are

required to converse with those little people so we can better appreciate how perfect we are." He holds up his beer to salute.

MaryJo blows off the comment, "I just think it's wonderful what we did and would love to find out how it affected him, that's all."

"Why does it matter? Isn't it enough that we helped him out? He's an adult who works hard and loves his family. Isn't it enough to know that we helped him? I'm sure he's feeling great!"

"Well that's true, but part of helping people out is looking at the joy in their smile, the optimism in their eyes and seeing the hope in humanity that people are good and do care." Maryjo counters.

"But you're looking for a payoff. You're the one who told me to do it anonymously. The joy of giving anonymously is simply in knowing that you helped them out. There shouldn't be any payoff."

"Well you make it sound like I'm a horrible person. I just thought maybe you saw him and wanted to know how he was doing, that's all."

Eric smiles at MaryJo, "I'm sure he's doing great MaryJo," as he takes a sip from his beer, then turns to Sue behind the bar, "Sue, ring the bell."

The bar has a bell that they ring whenever they want everyone's attention. Sue rings the bell as Eric stands up and turns to the main floor.

"Everybody who donated to the Christmas tree fund and help a family out, please stand up."

He pauses as a spattering of people stand.

"The rest of you hold up your drink and help me make a toast.' he pauses to let everyone raise their drinks, "To MaryJo, who came up with the idea, and to all these fine people standing who made it happen. Here's to the Christmas spirit!"

"TO THE CHRISTMAS SPIRIT!" the bar toasts.

"Now I want the servers to take note of those who are standing and make sure their next round is on my tab. Thank you all for helping out."

The patrons cheer as Eric returns to his seat, orders another round for both of them and turns to MaryJo, "There's your payoff, MaryJo."

MaryJo holds up her drink in salute to Eric, conceding the moment to her friend, "You're a good man Eric."

Eric responds without words, but simply by tapping his glass to hers in appreciation.

Meanwhile, Johnny has just entered and made his way to his seat next to Joe who has been quietly taking in the evening.

"Did I miss anything?" Johnny says as he settles into his seat.

Joe just smiles, "Not much. Just another night of our political duo proving once again that as much as we think we are different, the reality is we all have the same hearts."

Johnny smiles, "So what was the topic this time?"

"The family we helped out with a Christmas tree."

"Oh yes, how did that work out for them."

"Seemed to work out just fine, Johnny."

Sue brings a drink for both of them, "Johnny, Eric is buying your first drink for helping out with the tree." then she turns to Joe, "Eric's buying this one, but the rest of your drinks are on the house tonight."

Joe smiles, "Really?"

Sue looks at Joe with sincere gratitude, "You helped me keep my lights on. Buying your drinks is the least I can do."

Joe shakes his head, "Well young lady, on that night $142 dollars meant a whole lot more to you than it did me. I didn't do anything special. I just transferred some money from one place where it wasn't needed, to somewhere that it was needed. That's just good money management. But I'll tell you what I'll do. I'll pay for my drinks tonight if you'll find someone who could use a boost and let their tab be on the house instead. That's how you'll repay me. I helped you out in your time of need. You can help someone else out in their time of need. Who knows, maybe it will catch on"

Sue smiles, "Well it is the holiday season. I suspect there's a lot of people who could use a free bar tab."

Before she walks off, Joe stops her, "But here's the catch Sue ," she stops and turns back to him, "You have to tell me the story."

"Excuse me?"

"I trust your judgement. I'm sure everyone would love a free tab during the holidays. But I want you to find someone with a story that makes the free bar tab mean a lot more than just free booze. I want you to tell me about a free bar tab that touched a heart."

Sue looks at him admirably, yet a bit uncertain.

"I'm a writer, Sue. I love the stories. Go create one for me."

Sue accepts the challenge, "I'll let you know." as she heads off to fill another order.

Joe turns to Johnny, "So how's the Santa gig going?"

"Not bad. The usual. Kids asking for stuff they won't get, and parents encouraging me to promise them nothing."

"Have you come across any family I might be able to help?" Joe asks.

Johnny looks up at Joe as if a light just went on in his mind, "You know, come to think of it, I ate lunch today with a good friend I've known for years. He delivers the mail out that way and knows a lot about the families out there. I bet he would love to help out if you want."

"Perfect!" says Joe as he brightens with the thought, "The only thing I ask is that you be specific. I'm not giving someone $500 dollars if $400 dollars is enough. Make sure you find out what they actually need, and how much would be enough to help them out."

"I'm sure Pete can make a lot of families happy," says Johnny of his friend, "What kind of budget are we looking at?"

"Enough," says Joe with a smile, "As long as you ask for enough, I'll never say no. But I'll never give more than enough."

"Well I sure hope you sell a lot of books, because I'm

thinking Pete and I can help you spend that money." Says Johnny as he draws another sip from his drink.

Joe smiles, "Well don't you worry about me, Johnny. I always have enough. You just bring me the names and how much is enough to help them out, and I'll come by the next day with a nice card for your friend to deliver."

Johnny tips his drink with Joe's in a salute, "This could be a fun Christmas," he says with a twinkle in his eyes.

"Indeed. The best part of Christmas is in the giving enough to those in need."

As Sue delivers another round for the boys, she turns to Joe with enthusiasm, "I think I found your story Joe."

Joe perks up, "Excellent! What do you have?"

Sue leans in so only Joe and Johnny hears her, "See that guy at the other end of the bar? The one with the blue sweater?"

They both look, as Joe replies, "Yes, he comes here a lot."

Sue continues, "Yeah, he's a quiet guy. His name is Richard. A really good guy who likes to listen a lot more than talk. Anyways, I asked him how his Thanksgiving was and he hesitated before telling me his Mom passed away a few days before, so the family had to get together for Thanksgiving at her home, then had the funeral the next day. I've talked to him before and I know his family means a lot to him. His Mom was over 90 years old, but I'm still guessing it was a big loss to him."

Joe smiles in agreement, " Perfect! Richards heart could use a free bar tab a lot more than I could. Let me know if you need any help with his tab."

Sue looks at Joe defiantly, "No sir! This is one tab I'll be happy to pick up. It's Christmas and that's what the Christmas spirit is all about, right?"

Joe lovingly pats Sue on the cheek, "And that, my dear, is how you turn $142 dollars into a fortune."

Sue smiles in agreement as Johnny gets up to leave.

"Well those kids don't need to be sitting on the knees of an old Santa who's been up all night celebrating the Christmas spirit, that's for sure." he pats Joe on the back, "I'll see Pete tomorrow and recruit him for our Christmas give-away. You're a good man Joseph."

"Just remind him that it has to be enough and not a penny more."

"Will do, my friend. HoHoHo!" Johnny says in a loud voice signaling his exit.

5

_____

The Card

With Christmas two days away, life at the Pub seems to be more energized. Lots of laughter and upbeat conversations. Lots of last minute bags scattered about the floor and tables makes navigation a bit more challenging for the servers, but they don't mind as the festive atmosphere makes working this night worth the added effort.

Kim is working her tables with complete focus on the many details that make for good service, as Sue works the bar with the bright smile and attention to her customers that keeps the regulars at the bar coming back time and time again.

It's a good night at the bar. The events of the world have no place in tonight's bar as MaryJo and Eric seem much more agreeable in sharing their plans for the holiday than any political posturing.

Christmas music competes with the laughter and joy of the customers while Sue has 'It's a Wonderful Life' streaming on all the TVs, as it's the best Christmas movie to watch without sound because people have watched it so many times, they pretty much know it by heart.

As the festive mood carries the evening, Johnny makes his way to his seat, having worked a little later than normal. Johnny always has his Santa hat tucked into his trusty vest jacket pocket as if he wants to remind everyone of his role for the holidays. He could wear it, but that's too obvious for the more reserved Johnny, who always wears his old pidora hat anyway. Or he could leave it in the car, but the hat is always splashing over the pocket like a waterfall.

"Running a little behind, Johnny? Did you have to stop and feed the reindeer and get them ready for their big night?" Joe says as he orders a couple drinks from Sue, who is already delivering them and clearly doesn't need the order.

Johnny smiles, "Hell no. I don't feed them for a couple days. Don't want them to be too heavy, ya know. I tell them on Christmas Eve that we are going out to find the perfect pasture for them to eat all they want. That's how I get around so fast. The Reindeer are looking for the perfect pasture while I deliver all the toys."

Everyone loves how Johnny embraces his role as Santa. The rest of the year finds Johnny more reserved and unassuming. Lives alone and only speaks when spoken to. But when he plays Santa at Christmas, he's clearly more animated and bright.

"You really enjoy being Santa, don't you?" asks Joe

"It's a good way to spend the holidays for an old man like me." Johnny reflects as he takes a much needed sip.

"Will you be sad when it's over on Wednesday?"

"Naw, not really. I enjoy the holidays and talking to the kids, but I've had enough. It's time to move on to the peaceful quiet of winter."

"You're a smart man, Johnny boy. I've always felt the seasons were measured just right. I feel sorry for those who move to Florida so they can have 80 degrees all year long. I think 80 degrees feels so much better when it follows the frigid grips of winter."

Johnny holds up his glass, "I'll drink to that. 80 degrees, Summer only"

They tip their glasses in a toast, as Kim makes her way to the servers station for another round for table 17 that Sue is busily putting together for her.

Joe turns to Kim, "So Kim, you going home for Christmas?"

She replies as she organizes the drinks on her tray, "I am. It's only a couple hours drive and I just got an oil change for the old clunker, so it should be fine."

"Got a lot of family gathering?" asks Joe

"I do. My two sisters will be there and there is a good group of nieces and nephews to make it all worth the drive. Christmas is always special when there's kids around." she says.

Johnny lifts his glass to Kim, "I'll drink to that as well, young lady. To the children at Christmas."

Kim balances her load of drinks and as she heads for table 17, "Well you guys salute the children while I try to make some gas money tonight. I spent last week's tips buying gifts for those kids."

"You're a good woman, Kimberly." says Johnny in salute as she walks away.

As Johnny turns his attention back to the flow of the bar, Joe reflects as he signals Sue for another round.

"You know Johnny, we've done pretty good this holiday, don't you think?"

Johnny ponders with a delighted smile, "Indeed we have, Joseph."

"You and Pete helped some families have enough for their holidays. The bar has helped a couple families. Richard was comforted with a bar tab of love and support and Sue kept the lights on and her smile glowing brightly throughout the holidays. You know, there's a lot of people who say the Christmas spirit is dying, but I have $142 dollars that says it's alive a well."

Sue delivers their drinks, then lines up three shot glasses and fills them with her specialty holiday shot creation of lemonade, mango spirits and Gentleman Jack, then passes them out and lifts one for herself.

"To another great holiday at the Pub."

They toast, tap their shot on the bar counter and toss them down the hatch, before placing the shot glasses upside down on the bar.

As Sue moves on to the next customer, Joe turns to Johnny,

"So Johnny, do you think we missed anyone who needed help?"

Johnny shakes his head, "Well there is a lot of people who need help, ya know. But I think we got those who really needed a boost of Christmas spirit. We've done well."

"Well we still have a couple days to go, so if you come across anyone, you be sure and let me know." Joe says.

Johnny smiles, "Will do," as he takes another sip from his drink, obviously something is on his mind, "You know, Pete and I were talking about this guy who lives over that way, but we decided not to pass him along to you."

Joe perks up in curiosity, "Really? What's his story?"

"He's a good guy. Pete says his wife died last January from breast cancer. He got a pretty good life insurance payout and has a good job. He's a great Dad to his two little girls. We just feel that it must be hard for him right now. We feel sorry for him, that's all."

"Those are the people we should serve the most, Johnny." Joe says with a slight tone of disappointment.

"But he doesn't really need anything. You said to get specifics and only give then enough. He has enough. We couldn't see anything that we could do for him."

"Oh Johnny, giving has to come from your heart, not your wallet. It's easy to give money away, and if it helps others keep the lights on or comfort them in their time of loss, that's great. Money is just a tool. A hammer is a great tool, but only if you need to build a wall. This young man doesn't need our money, you're correct about that, but what he does need is so much more important to the spirit of the holidays than any amount of money. He needs a hug. He needs to know that we see him and feel for him and what he's going through. He needs to know that he is never alone and as long as he keeps his heart open to the love that surrounds him, he'll always have enough in life."

Joe reaches into his coat pocket and pulls out a card, then turns to Sue and asks her to ring the bell. Sue rings the bell as she turns down the holiday music.

"Ladies and gentlemen, I'm sorry to interrupt your festive celebrations, but it has come to my attention that we have a man who lives in this community who needs our help. This man lost his wife to cancer last January and this will be his first Christmas without her. He's doing fine financially, so he doesn't need our money. He's a single Dad with two precious little girls to look after. As we enjoy a wonderful evening of holiday spirits with our friends, he is likely sitting alone, the girls tucked into bed, feeling the weight of sadness as he misses his wife. I want each of you to come up to the bar and sign this card for him. Just sign your name, no message. He likely will not know any of the names on this card, but what he will know is that he lives in a community that cares. What he will know is that he's never alone. What he will know is that we see what he is going through. And he will know that we think he's a good Dad and if he leaves his heart open to the many possibilities of LOVE, he will always have enough in life. Please." he says as he lays the card out.

As Joe starts to sit back in his seat, Sue rings the bell again.

"And let me just add, that when you come up to the bar to sign this card, let me know what you are drinking because it's on the house, baby!!"

Sue cranks up the holiday music and begins to sing with it, 'Joy to the World….' as people make their way to the bar to sign the card, many with tissues in hand from the emotions of the moment, and many singing along as well.

Joe turns to Johnny as Sue delivers another drink, "It's never about the money Johnny, it's always about the love. This card will help this young man feel strong during a difficult time. You never put a price tag on that."

Johnny salutes Joe by raising his glass, "I'll make sure Pete delivers it to him personally tomorrow. You're a good man Joseph!"

As Joe gets up to head out, Kim makes her way to the servers station. "Well it certainly got festive in here, right Kim?" says Joe

"Damn, Joe, you really know how to get a party going. I'll make enough tonight not only for gas, but maybe a couple bottles of Champaign for the adults."

Joe laughs as he puts on his coat, "Well then, " he hands Kim a ten dollar bill, "Pick up some orange juice, too. Christmas morning without mimosas is unimaginable."

"Thanks, Joe! Have a great Christmas!" says Kim with a hug.

"You too, young lady." as he turns to Johnny, "You'll take care of the card then?"

Johnny assure him, "Absolutely. Pete's going to love this delivery."

Joe waves his arm with a "Merry Christmas everyone!" and as he heads out the door, many voices can be heard, "Merry Christmas Joe!"

6

The Car

As the holiday decorations seem to be sagging a bit, the Pub seems to be much more relaxed and quieter than a few days earlier before Christmas. No more shopping bags to work around, as the population of the bar quickly returns to the neighborhood hang out that the regulars appreciate the rest of the year. They have no problem getting their regular seat at the bar, and the conversations no longer have to compete with the hustle and bustle of a frantic holiday energy.

It's a recovery time for most. They have survived the stress and emotional drama consistent with the family holiday and they welcome the quieter, more comforting surroundings of just another night at the local Pub.

Johnny has his regular place next to the servers station, MaryJo and Eric are close by. Richard quietly settles in at the other end of the bar as Sue tends to his needs for quenching his thirst. Kim is working the tables with much less urgency tonight as there is just enough people gathered about to make for a calm working environment. A nice break from the past couple of weeks. As Kim makes her way to the servers station, Sue heads over to fill her order for table 10 as Johnny is quick to visit with the girls.

"Did you girls have a nice Christmas?"

Sue responds first, "It was nice. Having the day off and to myself was enough for me. How was your trip to your family?" she asks Kim, who suddenly perks up.

"Oh, get this. I go outside on Christmas morning to head down to my parents and sitting behind my car was a brand new car with a bow on it and a card that said 'To Kim'."

Sue screams as Johnny nearly falls off his stool in response to the sudden scream he was not ready for.

"You're kidding!!" blasts Sue with great enthusiasm, "Someone gave you a new car?!?!?!"

"Yeah, but I don't have any idea who did it!" as she pulls out a card from her pocket, "Here, this is all I got."

The card was simple. On the outside it read, 'If you ask for more, you'll never have enough', then on the inside, it reads, 'If you ask for enough, you'll never need more'. No signature, no notes. "This is all I had and a key inside the envelope."

Sue is amazed, "Do you have it here? I want to see it!"

Kim stops, "Oh hell no! I'm not touching that thing until I know who gave it to me and why."

"You didn't take it down to your parents?" Sue says.

"Hey, there's a lot of creeps out there, ya know."

"But it's Christmas, " Sue counters, "Someone gave you

a new car because they knew you needed one. That's not creepy, that's pretty nice."

Kim turns to Johnny, "Well what do you think, Santa Clause? Were you in on this?"

Johnny laughs, "Oh sweetheart, I give kids watermelons, I don't do new cars." he says even though he notices that the card she has is the same card Joe has been giving him and Pete during the holidays, so he has a pretty good idea where the car came from. "Maybe you should appreciate the gift and stop worrying about the source?"

"I can't do that. A bottle of perfume is a gift, but a brand new car is another story. That's a huge investment. I can't accept it without knowing who gave it to me and why."

"Did Eric's friend know who made his Christmas special?' says Johnny, "Did the single parent know who gave him the card of encouragement? The spirit of Christmas is about giving to others. Everyone knows your car sucks and how great it is that someone was in a position to give you a new car. Whoever did it doesn't matter, what matters is that there are many people in this bar who wish they were in a position to do so because they love you. Just accept it."

"But that's way more than anyone else got Johnny."

"Oh Kim, I would argue that a single Dad a few miles east of here got a lot more than you this Christmas. It's not about the money, Kim, it's about the heart."

Kim pauses with tears welling up in her eyes, "But I don't deserve such a gift."

"Well maybe it's time for you to look at yourself a little

closer, Kim." Johnny says as he holds her chin in his hand with a deep smile of compassion, " I'm Santa after all, Kim, and you're not on the naughty list, ya know."

With that, Kim crumbles into Johnny's arms as the floodgates open. Sue is quick to rescue the drinks and head them over to table 10 and Eric raises his glass for another toast.

"To Kim. The best damn server this side of Pluto."

Everyone cheers as Kim has a good cry on Johnny's shoulder.

MaryJo looks to Eric, "This side of Pluto?"

Eric looks defensively at her, "Yeah. Well they don't know what's on the other side of Pluto ya know. Too much?"

MaryJo smiles at Eric as she considers her response, yet comes up empty, "No. It wasn't too much. It was perfect."

Eric sits back in a proud posture, smiling, as MaryJo turns to Sue returning from table 10, "Sue, how about another round for us, please."

"Coming up." says Sue.

After she serves Eric and MaryJo, Sue makes her way back to the servers station and hands out 3 shots for her, Kim and Johnny, "Here's to the Christmas spirit." They tap their glasses and toss back the spirits as Sue quickly gathers the empty glasses to take away any evidence that anyone would be drinking on the job.

"Now get yourself together and go hit those tables, dearie. Your car insurance just doubled."

They all break into laughter as Kim quickly wipes away

her tears and straightens out her persona, then looks to Johnny again.

"I know you know who did it and I hope you let them know how deeply appreciative I am for their kindness."

"I'm sure they already know. I'm sure that's why they did it."

"I'm still not comfortable accepting it, though"

"Ah Kimberly. Most people struggle to accept gifts of kindness with no strings attached. It's hard for people to simply appreciate the gift and say thank you."

"But I can't say thank you if I don't know who to thank."

" Sure you can," Johnny says, "You can thank them by being kinder to your customers. By having a more positive presence in your daily walk. By working harder in school and becoming an even better version of yourself every day. People love to give to others anonymously. Look at how much this bar got into the Christmas spirit this year. That's okay. Hell that's why I love being Santa. Helping the kids out without them knowing it's from me. Who doesn't enjoy that? What's important is knowing that whoever gave you that car is feeling really good today because they were able to help a friend out. You say thank you by giving to others anonymously whenever you have the opportunity."

Kim shakes her head, conceding all she has heard, "I guess it was a pretty good Christmas for a lot of people hasn't it Johnny?"

As Kim heads out to start working her tables, Sue comes

over to the servers station to take advantage of a slow break and start cleaning some glasses stacking up at the station.

"It was Joe, wasn't it?" she asks Johnny.

"Well I wasn't in on it of course, but I'm guessing he'd be a pretty good bet."

"You know I tried to Google him to see what he's written and there is not one person here who even knows his last name. I can't just Google 'Joe, the writer' Do you know?"

Johnny shakes his head, "I don't. I just know him as Joe. I asked him if he had a family once, and he said he had lots of family. Everywhere he goes he has family. You just can't get into his personal life. Some people are just private like that. But he must be a pretty good writer because Pete and I gave him a lot of families to help out and he didn't say no to any of them. We spent a lot of his money this holiday season, and he never blinked."

Sue wipes her hands as she heads to a new patron sitting at the bar, "Maybe he's the real Santa and he's just checking up on you."

Johnny smiles as he takes another sip from his drink as MaryJo calls out to Johnny, "So Santa, it sounds like you had a pretty good Christmas, huh?"

"It was indeed. The Christmas spirit is alive and well. Looks like a lot of people got help who really needed it."

"That's nice. I always feel a little let down after Christmas. I wish the Christmas spirit could last throughout the year."

Eric rolls his eyes, as Johnny jumps in quickly to avoid another debate, "I think it does, MaryJo."

"You're kidding. Have you watched the news lately? I don't see much Christmas spirit during the rest of the year, that's for sure."

"Ah Maryjo, the evening news pays their rent by selling fear, chaos and danger. It gives people like you and Eric plenty of ammunition to debate in bars all over the country. But if you pay attention to the actual world we live in, you'll see people stepping up every time there's a disaster and helping out. Hurricanes in the Gulf coast, tornados in the mid-section, fires out west, blizzards in the east, you will always find neighbors helping neighbors, regardless of the color of their skin or what church they go to. Just neighbors recognizing the needs of other neighbors, stepping up and pitching in. I see the Christmas spirit all the time."

Eric raises his glass, "I'll drink to that Johnny!"

MaryJo continues, "Well I wish the news would report those stories more."

Eric is quick to reply, "Well it's the liberal media that creates the doomsday atmosphere, you know."

Before MaryJo can reply, Johnny tells Sue to ring the bell. The room becomes silent as everyone draws their attention to Johnny, who is getting out of his seat, having put his money on the counter and is adjusting his coat around his shoulders as he acknowledges the others anticipation for what he rang the bell for.

He smiles, "Oh, I got nothing. Have a nice evening everyone."

As he leaves, Eric, MaryJo, Sue and the others burst into

laughter, realizing Johnny's masterful style of killing the debate.

7

The Exit

As the deep freeze of winter chills the energy of life from our small suburban community, life at the Pub is much more quiet and relaxed. Football season has been put to bed as the Pubs TVs only get a spattering of attention with it's menu of basketball and hockey games in midseason form drawing little interest from sports fans who understand those sports still have a few months before they become noteworthy.

As Kim waits at the servers station for Sue to gather up another round for table 8, Johnny seizes the opportunity to start the conversation. "So Kim, how's that new car working out for you?"

"Good. I even had a professor tell me that he noticed I've been getting to class on time now." she says as she organizes her round for table 8.

"Excellent. Good to hear the little act of kindness helped you become a better version of yourself." Johnny says, as he takes another sip from his drink.

Kim laughs, "Oh Johnny, a little act of kindness is when someone picks up the tab for someone who is struggling. Buying a brand new car for a casual acquaintance is a hell of a lot more than a little act of kindness. It's like calling the Titanic a fender-bender."

Johnny smiles and shakes his head, "Ah Kimberly, you can never measure an act of kindness by it's finances. I would argue that a wealthy person buying you a new car isn't nearly as impressive as a simple Christmas card signed by a bunch of strangers."

Kim, never one to easily back down from her opinions, "That may be so, but I'm just say'n no matter how wealthy that person may be, buying me a new car was a very generous act of kindness. You're right about the money, but there are a lot of wealthy people who only give to others when they need a tax break. The impressive thing about buying me that car is not the wallet it came from, but the heart it came from. Now that's a big heart." she says as she heads for table 8.

Johnny smiles as he holds his drink up to Kim, "That's the lesson, Kim…. that is the lesson."

Meanwhile, Sue delivers another round to MaryJo and Eric and is anxious to stir things up, "Did you guys see where the Football Commissioner and Players Union President are arguing over the rules for the national anthem? You'd think that with all the injury time outs making a 60 minute game last nearly 4 hours, they'd have more important things to talk about."

MaryJo is quick to grab the bait, "Oh, don't think for a

minute that the Commissioner is the least bit worried about injury time outs. If the game lasts four hours, that just means a whole lot more revenue from the beer and chip advertisers."

Eric picks up the pace, "They've come a long way in protecting the athletes, it's just a violent game of contact that America loves to watch. They can only do so much about the injuries."

"Oh please," as MaryJo almost chokes on her drink, "Come a long way? That's a joke! I challenge you that if you look at a picture of a football player from the 70s and a picture from today, you can't tell me they are making any progress for the safety of their athletes. Hell, you can clearly see the gender of these boys, their uniforms are so tight. And they clearly have no protection. Safety is of no concern to the NFL."

"Well now we know why you take such an interest in the game, MaryJo." says Eric with a hint of smugness at landing a solid punch.

"Ha, ha, ha. My point is that NASCAR understood that it was not okay when they saw their most popular driver die in a violent crash at Daytona and they did something about it. They made their sport even better because the fans now love to watch the races knowing that most anytime there is a violent crash, their favorite drivers will be climbing out of their cars flipping off the other driver that made them crash. NASCAR clearly cares about their drivers. The NFL would rather talk about the national anthem. They don't care about their players."

"Oh Maryjo, they're working on the safety of their players

a lot more than you and other liberals want to admit. Besides, the national anthem issue is important. You have a bunch of athletes who children look up to, who make a lot of money and live a very comfortable living and they choose to show their appreciation by taking a knee during our countries anthem? I think they should rip up their contracts and let them go work in a factory if that's how they feel."

MaryJo nearly spits out her drink, "What!?! The ability to protest is what makes our country so great! There is not one word in the constitution that says we have to behave a certain way during the national anthem. Freedom has to be for everyone regardless of what the elite may think about it. It's okay to burn a flag when you are protesting our county's involvement in wars. It's okay to gather in protest and demand justice for all no matter how much you may disagree with it. But you have one black man quietly take a knee in protest during a football game and everyone goes crazy and demonizes the guy as a horrible American. If you ask me, that young man showed a lot more respect for what our country stands for than all those people who are whining about it now do."

Eric shakes his head, "Oh, go hug a tree, Maryjo. It's your attitude and liberal thinking that screws this country up. Freedom is for all, but you have to have some regulations and rules or those freedoms get way out of control and do nothing more than create absolute chaos."

"Typical right-wing thinking, Eric. You scream so loud at any thought of regulating our banks and businesses of the elite, yet when it comes to giving freedoms to our rank and file people, you scream for regulations. You say they simply made some poor judgements when the greedy banks drove our country into a difficult recession, yet when a black man quietly takes a knee, you scream a moral message of what a horrible role model these athletes are to our children. Let's be clear, the athlete taking a knee is a much better role model to our children than any Wall Street CEO, that's for sure."

Eric shakes his head in frustration, "There is a big difference between the freedoms of commerce and the freedoms of civil behavior, that's for sure." turns to Sue, "I'm ready for another beer, Sue."

"There's only a difference in the eyes of the greedy." she too engages Sue, "I'll have another as well."

The debate comes to an abrupt stop as Joe comes through the door and makes his way towards the seat next to Johnny. It's been since before Christmas that Joe has dropped into the Pub, so there is an air of excitement mixed in with concern as Joe seems a bit taken back at all the attention his presence has created.

"We were starting to think you forgot about us, Joe." says Sue as she quickly delivers a drink to his spot.

"I would never forget this fine group of people. Been out of town on some business, that's all." says Joe, "Did I miss anything while I was gone?" he says in order to turn the spotlight away from himself as he is always prone to do.

Sue is quick to respond, "Some secret admirer gave Kim

a new car for Christmas that she's dying to find out who it was."

Joe takes a sip from his drink, then responds, "Well that won't be too easy as I suspect Ms Kim has many secret admirers in her world."

As Kim makes her way back to the servers station for another order, she turns to Joe, "I suppose you have no idea who the angel was, do you?"

Joe pauses in thought as he takes a sip before responding, "Well Kim, I imagine there are many angels with enough appreciation for you that would have been delighted to help you out with a new car for Christmas. Besides, this guy here is Santa Clause. If he doesn't know who the angel was, I'm guessing nobody else would know." he says as he toasts Johnny.

"Well it's hard to say thank you to someone you don't know." says Kim as she loads up her tray.

"Not so, young lady," says Joe emphatically, "Your smile says thank you enough. You keep that smile going for everyone you meet and you'll know that you have said thank you to whoever the angel was that helped you out."

She shakes her head a bit frustrated as she heads to deliver the load of drinks. Anyone who knows Joe, knows they are not going to get much out of him, that's for sure.

"So Johnny, how's the world without Santa Clause treating you, my friend?"

"Not too bad. You know, Kim showed us the card she got with her car, and it was the same card you were giving Pete and I for all the families we helped through the holiday, so I pretty much figured it out. But I didn't say anything."

"Aw, I don't worry about that, Johnny. Kim got a new car, your single Dad got a special card – only one letter separates the two. The main thing is that they both got enough, right?"

Johnny lifts his glass to salute Joe, "You're a good man, Joe."

They tip their glasses as Joe continues, "Speaking of good men, have you heard much about your single Dad?"

Johnny perks up, "Yeah, actually he came into the Pub about a month ago."

"You're kidding. He figured out who gave him the card?"

"Yeah, he said he knew one of the names on the card and knew she had talked about the Pub from time to time. He had often wanted to drop by and check us out, but never had the time to do so, but with his girls staying at their grandparents, he had to come by and check it out."

"Well he is a single parent, I guess," Joe confirms.

Johnny takes another pull from his glass and signals Sue for another round for the both of them as he continues.

"Once it was revealed that this was indeed the origin of the card, it became quite a scene of hugs, tears of gratitude and rounds being bought by everyone. Quite a night."

Joe smiles as the fresh drinks are delivered and they both raise their glasses.

"You know, it's a great day when people learn that giving has nothing to do with money. Look at all the people who were helped this holiday. It's not about how much was spent, it's a matter of knowing that people received enough to make it a great holiday for everyone. You can't put a price tag on giving as long as you always give enough." Joe says.

Johnny takes a sip and considers what Joe says, "We were able to help a lot of people this year, Joe" Johnny looks at Joe, "Is that why you've been out of action lately? Been eating beans 'n wieners the past few months trying to get your budget back on track?"

Joe looks at Johnny with an unforgiving look of hesitancy as Johnny smiles and responds, "I know, it's not about the money. But you have to admit that we spent a lot of your money this holiday."

"Yes we did. And I would argue that the best gift we gave this year was the card to a single parent. And that didn't cost us a dime." Joe responds.

Kim makes her way back to the servers station and calls to Sue, who comes over, "See that couple over there at table 4? The lady just found out she has breast cancer. Whatever they order tonight, put it on my tab and I'll square up with you after my shift." as Sue looks at the order and agrees with Kim

"You see, Kim. That's how you say thank you." says Joe who overheard the conversation.

"Oh Joe, I'm pretty sure everyone has figured out that you were my Santa Clause this year." she looks at him in deep appreciation, "Thank You."

"Well Kim, that doesn't matter. What matters is that you understand that words will never say thank you more than what you're doing for table 4. Do me a favor and get me the name of the young lady, would you?"

"Oh no you don't Joe. I'm picking up the tab for them tonight, not you." Kim says emphatically.

"I said nothing about picking up their tab, young lady. I happen to know some experts in the field who might be able to help her out, but I'll need a lot more than just saying the lady at table 4 needs your help. She must have a name." says Joe with a smile.

Kim backs down and smiles, "Okay Joe, I'll get her name. But her tab is mine."

Joe raises his glass to Kim, "Good. I hope they order steak from the kitchen." he says as Kim is not phased, "Me too. The group at table 8 was very generous tonight. I'll even push the steak for them." Kim smiles as she takes another round out to her customers.

Johnny, who has been quietly listening to the banter between the two, finally speaks up, "So you know doctors who can cure cancer too?" he says with a hint of disbelief.

Joe smiles at his tone, "What can I say, Johnny, I'm a writer you know. I meet a lot of people with interesting stories."

Johnny has learned not to pursue topics of a personal nature with Joe, so he simply lifts his glass to acknowledge and takes a sip, while Joe continues.

"Speaking of writing, I came by tonight to say goodbye for a bit, " as Johnny looks over to Joe, who continues, "I have another assignment that will take me away for some time, but I wanted to thank you for your help through the holidays."

"What kind of assignment?" asks Johnny, realizing he probably won't get much of an answer.

"Oh just another story. Another chapter in the story of life. It's going to take me away for some time, but I'm sure you all will survive without me. But I also wanted to let you know about a friend of mine that may contact you. His name is George Geta. Good guy. Anyway, if you are contacted by a guy named George Geta, listen to what he has to say, he's a good guy with a good story."

Johnny looks a bit confused, "Will he come here to the bar?"

Joe hesitates, "I'm not sure, to be honest. I've never seen him with a drink. He should though. A bit on the stressed side, if you ask me, but he has a lot of responsibilities, so I let it go. But I think the two of you would hit it off nicely, so if you cross paths, be sure and listen to what he has to say, would you?"

Johnny knows he is not likely to get much more from Joe and simply responds, "Sure."

As Kim comes back, she stops Joe who is getting up to leave, "Hey, I found out that ladies name is Carol Farthing. I told her we know some people around here who might be able to help her out."

Joe smiles, "Excellent." he looks at Kim, "Did they order the steak?"

Kim smiles, "They sure did baby, and I'm making sure it comes with the works!"

"That's my girl. Paying it forward is the best way to say thank you. That's what it's all about."

Joe turns to Johnny to simply say, "Take care Johnny boy, take care."

And with that, Joe leaves the Pub for the last time.

8

———

The Nurse

As Winters chilling bite gives way to the rebirth of natures Spring bursting all about, life at the Pub also turns it's attention to a new season of baseball, outdoor activities and general renewal of spirits. In Winter, people in these parts simply do what they have to do to survive, but once Springtime makes it's presence known, people are anxious to get out more and create more than just a survival existence. The mood is always upbeat in the Spring.

As Kim makes her way to the servers station, Johnny notices her upbeat presence.

"You seem to be in good spirits tonight, Kim."

"Why not, Johnny. I just graduated from nursing school, took my boards and am feeling pretty good about that, and I already have an offer from the local hospital as soon as I get my license. There's a lot to be upbeat about." she says as she loads her tray of another round for table 6.

"Nurse Kim. I like it." says Johnny in approval.

"The only down side is I'll likely have to give up my shifts at the Pub and only work now and then when they need an extra hand." as she heads to table 6.

Sue delivers another drink to Johnny who continues the conversation, only with a different set of ears, "That's pretty good news about Kim, don't you think?"

"Well she hasn't received the scores from her boards yet, but anyone who knows Kim knows that she aced it. When that girl sets her sights on something, you don't bet against her, that's for sure."

"Yeah, I sure wouldn't bet against Kimberly for anything." Johnny says in agreement, "So what kind of nursing does she want to do?"

"Not sure. She's talked a lot about traveling the world and if she's a good enough nurse, she would have no problems getting work wherever she goes."

Johnny smiles, "The two jobs you can always find anywhere in the world is nursing and bars. I would say Kimberly has set herself up nicely."

As Sue moves on to another customer, a man walks into the Pub and takes the seat next to Johnny. He is not a familiar face. He looks around as if looking for someone in particular.

Sue approaches him, "What can I get you?"

The man looks over the rows of options, when a scream comes from behind.

" DAD!" yells Kim in excitement, " What are you doing here?" Then she looks at Sue, "This is my dad and he'll have a

Jack 'n Coke – make it a double!" then turns back to her dad, "So what brings you down here?"

Kims dad smiles at her, "Well it just seemed like a good idea that when your daughter finds out she passed the boards with flying colors, her dad should probably be there to buy her the first drink."

" WHAT?!" says Kim as her dad pulls a letter from his jacket pocket and hands it to her.

Kim looks at the letter and screams with full throttle excitement as her dad looks to Johnny who is obviously blown away from the scream.

"You'll have to excuse my daughter, " he says with a proud smile, "She got a really good score on her boards."

Johnny smiles and salutes him with his drink as Sue delivers the Jack 'n Coke.

"How did you get this?" Kim says to her dad.

"Apparently, you never updated your records when you moved out, so they sent it to us. I opened it because if it was bad news, I was just going to mail it back to you with a comforting note, but if it was good news I was definitely going to deliver that in person."

Kim smothers her dad with a big hug as Sue goes over and rings the bell and waits for everyone's attention before speaking.

"As most of you know, Kim has been working hard here at the Pub as she went through nursing school. She just found out from her dad, " turns to him, "You do have a name, right?" He surfaces from the smothering hug to respond breathlessly, "Jack" "Kims dad, Jack, just brought her the scores from her boards and you are all welcome to call her Nurse Kim from now on." she holds up a shot, "To Nurse Kim!"

"NURSE KIM" the bar responds in unison, as Sue rings the bell in celebration.

As the mood settles into its normal calm chaos, Kim gathers herself and encourages her dad to stay put while she delivers another round. As Kim gathers up the drinks for table 4, Johnny moves the conversation to Jack.

"So Kim is your daughter? She's a fine young lady, Jack. You've done well." He raises his glass as Jack responds in kind.

"She is indeed. She's gonna be a hell of a nurse, too." Jack says.

As Johnny and Jack chit chat at the end of the bar, MaryJo has made her way to the seat next to Eric, who is quick to start the conversation.

"Hey Lefty, I met your husband the other day at the office. Marty, right? He came by the office for something and when I realized he was your husband, we got to talking a bit. He's not nearly the crazy liberal that you are." he says with a smile which MaryJo just ignores.

"He's a good man and a great husband. He's one of the few conservatives on this planet that actually listens and considers my point of view. I think there's hope for Marty. In the meantime, it gives me great pleasure to go to the polls every election and cancel out his vote." she says with a keen sense of smugness.

Meanwhile, Johnny and Jack take in a good laugh in their conversation as Sue delivers a shot for the two men.

"So Jack, How long are you staying in town?" she asks as the two slam their shots down the hatch.

"Oh probably not long. A good dad knows better than to wear out your welcome. I'm sure Kim has plenty of friends around here to celebrate her new life without the old man hanging around."

"Well everyone loves your daughter, Jack. You should be proud of her." says Sue

"No question about it. She's a bull-headed, determined young lady, that's for sure, but she's always been able to channel that stubborn energy into positive work, so I never tried to hold her back. I'm lucky to have such a daughter. She's going to help a lot of people, I'm guessing."

As he takes a sip from his drink, he looks at Sue, "Guess she'll probably have to leave here, though, right?" he asks as Sue gathers the shot glasses and shakes her head.

"Don't want to think about it. She will be missed for sure, but as long as people leave for the right reasons, you have to just let them go."

Sue moves on as Kim comes back to the station. "Hey dad, the manager just cut me for the evening so I can visit with you." she says excitedly, " Maybe we can grab a table , have dinner and I'll fill you in on my new job."

"That'd be great. "

Kim turns to Johnny with a long face, "Is that okay with you, Johnny ? I hate to take away your conversation."

Johnny smiles, "By all means, Kim. I'm sure he's had enough of my conversations. You can have him all to yourself." he turns to Jack, "I'm not sure what the fellas do back there in the kitchen, but their fried chicken is pretty good stuff if you don't have a doctors appointment any time soon." he tells him.

Jack laughs and holds up his drink to Johnny, "Thanks Johnny, maybe the next time. Tonight I'm buying my girl a great steak with the works and a bottle of her favorite wine!"

"Bottle of Merlo for table 2" shouts Kim to Sue, as she grabs her dad's arm and continues, "Come on dad, I got us table 2 because it's the best table in the Pub for talking."

With that, Kim and Jack move on to table 2 as Sue delivers a bottle of their best Merlo.

Meanwhile, Johnny sits alone debating whether he should have another drink or call it a night as a man comes walking into the Pub and looks around. A simple man with nothing that draws much attention to him, he sees Johnny and decides to take the seat next to him.

"Mind if I take this seat?" he asks Johnny.

Johnny looks at him and smiles, "It's not mine to give away, but if you just want to sit a spell, you're welcome to take up residence there tonight."

He sits down and orders a drink from Sue, then turns to Johnny, "Is your name Johnny?" he asks.

Johnny perks up curiously. "Yes it is. And you are?"

"George Geta. A friend of mine said I might find you at the end of the bar here."

Johnny interrupts, "Ah yes. Joe told me I might come across a guy named George Geta and if I did, I was to listen to him."

George takes a sip from the drink Sue just delivered and continues, "Yes, Joe and I have worked many projects together."

Johnny again interrupts, "Ah, another writer. So what kind of research are you doing?"

George hesitates, "Well I'm not a writer, I run a non-profit near by and Joe has done some work for me. He told me about you and this Pub."

Johnny doesn't hesitate to jump in again, "When Joe told me to look out for you, I asked him if you would be coming by the bar. He looked at me a bit confused and said he wasn't sure. He'd never seen you with a drink in your hand, so he wasn't sure if you'd be coming by the Pub or not."

George smiles, yet gets a bit defensive, "How would he know, he's always out doing research. The only time he sees me is at my office from time to time and he gives me attitude that I work too hard and I need to get out more. He thinks I live there."

Johnny laughs as Sue delivers another drink, the decision to stay being settled when George walked in.

"So Joe says I need to listen to you, so what can I do for you? I do hope it's not a time share deal or anything like that." he says as he takes a sip of his beverage.

George nearly chokes on his drink, "Oh lord no." he says, then pauses, "But if you've been talking to Joe, I can see where you'd get that idea, I suppose. He seems like the kind that would love a time share don't you think?."

They both toast in agreement before George continues.

"No, nothing like a time share. As I mentioned before, I run a non-profit and am always looking for recruits, so Joe likes to pass along names of people he thinks would be a good fit when he's out researching."

"What kind of program you running?" asks Johnny, happy to know it's not going to be a high pressure sales pitch.

"Oh this is not the place to explain it, " he pulls out a rather plain business card that simply says GETA Foundation and has the address, "Come by tomorrow and I'll give you all the details in my office." and hands the card to Johnny, who looks at it somewhat unimpressed.

"Nice card." he says with a slight tone of sarcasm.

"Well it is a non-profit after all. It has the name and address and that's all you need for now. Once you come by, I'll give you the whole rundown and see what you think."

"Out of curiosity, what is it about me that you and Joe think I'd be a great prospect?" Johnny asks.

"He says you play Santa Clause for the kids every Christmas and have a good heart." George says as he takes another sip.

"Well I'm not sure about the heart – I am 85 ya know- but I do spend my holidays being Santa, I suppose. I'm not getting younger and I do enjoy my quiet retirement, so whatever you've got going, don't count on me for anything that takes up a lot of time and energy."

"Oh don't worry about that. Trust me, if you're interested in our program, we'll make sure it's a perfect fit for you." George says, hoping that the conversation will stop there and move onto something else.

Fortunately, Johnny lays some cash on the counter and gets up to leave. "So what time do you want me to come by tomorrow?" he says to George.

"So you're going to come by tomorrow?" he says somewhat surprised.

Johnny smiles, "Well I am retired. It's not like I have to rearrange my schedule or anything. Besides, Joe's a mysterious guy, but he really is a good man. If he says I need to listen to what you have to say, I'm thinking he wouldn't be steering me wrong. I'll be happy to hear you out."

"Let's make it around 10?" George says.

"Sounds good," says Johnny as he turns to Sue who was bringing another drink for him.

"I'm beat, young lady. I think it's time to go home and quietly read my book."

"Okay Johnny. We'll see you later."

With that, a spattering of farewells come from around the bar as Johnny heads out the door.

Meanwhile, Sue offers the drink to George. "No charge for this one, " she says as she puts it in front of him.

He shrugs, "Why not. I'm told I don't get out enough."

"So you're a friend of Joe? How's he doing? We miss him coming in around here?"

"Seems to be doing well, I suppose. I only see him now and then, but he's always doing well." he says.

Sue smiles, "He's always doing research, you mean. That guy never talks about himself. Kind of a private guy, yet during the holidays there was no one as generous as Joe. He sure has a big heart."

"He does indeed," George agrees.

"Well any friend of Joe is always welcome here, so don't be a stranger." Sue says as she moves off to serve a new customer, leaving George alone at the end of the bar to take in the life that is the Pub.

9

The Daughter

It's a quiet night at the Pub, most of the noise coming from the baseball games being offered on the monitors about the place. All the regulars seem to be a bit subdued with little conversation going on as Sue cleans glasses behind the bar.

MaryJo enters and breaks the heavy atmosphere. She is holding some flowers which she lays down near the servers station, where Johnny would be sitting if he was there. She seems upset and anxious as she takes the seat next to Eric. "I just heard about it today. What happened?"

Sue stops her work to respond, "They found him in his favorite chair with a book in his lap. Said he'd been gone for a couple of days."

"Oh my word. He was here a couple of days ago and seemed like the usual Johnny. It must of happened right after that." says MaryJo as Sue delivers her a drink.

"He did seem a bit tired. He even told me before he left that he was beat and ready to go sit and read his book." says Sue as she grabs a tall beer mug, fills it with water and heads over to give the flowers a new home at Johnny's spot.

"Did they say how he died?" asks MaryJo who always wants all the details.

Of course, Eric is always willing to jump on MaryJo's comments, "He was 85. sitting in his favorite chair reading a good book. Cause of death – Time!" he says as he lifts his glass.

"Well you don't have to make light of it, Eric." says MaryJo somewhat annoyed at his tone.

"I'm not making light of it, Maryjo, I'm celebrating Johnny. Hell, I hope when my time comes that I can be sitting in my favorite chair reading a good book, that's for sure. I'm going to miss him as much as the rest of you, but I am not willing to disrespect him by sitting around moping about it. I'm going to celebrate his life and the fact that I was lucky enough to know him."

With that, Sue starts lining up a bunch of shot glasses and filling them with her special recipe and rings the bell.

"The Pub has lost a very dear friend. We will all miss Johnny for sure. But tonight we celebrate Johnny who is now with the love of his life, Beth." she passes out the shot glasses until everyone at the bar has one before continuing, lifting her glass.

" To Johnny! Thank you for all you did for us at the Pub, for all the kids you helped out during the holidays…"

Suddenly a voice surfaces from behind them by the door, " And all you did for me as a dad."

Everything comes to a screeching halt as the regulars turn to find a woman in her mid to late 50s standing with tears in her eyes, holding a familiar Santa hat in her hands.

"I wasn't sure if I had the right place, but now I'm pretty sure this is the place my dad talked about. Mind if I join you?"

As she approaches the bar, everyone is stunned and have no idea how they should respond, while Sue quickly sets up another shot as the visitor continues.

"Knowing my dad and the look on your faces, I'm guessing he didn't talk a lot about his personal life." she smiles, "I was thinking as I was coming in that if this is the right place, it's likely they had no idea that Johnny had a daughter. My name is Elizabeth. Named after my mom. Dad always got a kick out of that. He'd tell me that it was baffling how boys were named after their dad, but why aren't girls named after their mom? So he talked mom into letting me be named Elizabeth" she turns to Sue, "Anyway, I'm sorry I interrupted you … you were toasting my dad?"

Sue looks around at all the regulars who are still lost for words and then back to Elizabeth, holding up her glass.

"To Johnny. A good friend, a good dad, and a damn good Santa!"

"TO JOHNNY" as they all take their shots and Sue rings the bell in celebration, then turns to Elizabeth.

"What can I get you Elizabeth?"

"A Tom Collins, please."

Sue perks up, "Oh my God, you are his daughter. That's what I fixed Johnny every time he came in."

Elizabeth smiles, "I learned a lot from my dad."

MaryJo finally breaks the ice of the frozen regulars, "How did we not know Johnny had a daughter?"

Eric quickly replies, "I never asked him about that stuff. He was always just Johnny, the old man at the end of the bar. That was always enough for me."

"Well what kind of friends are we if we don't know a thing about him. Does anyone know what he retired from? What he did for a living?" MaryJo asks

"Maybe he was a full time Santa. He seemed pretty good at that." says Eric in an attempt to give light to the air of embarrassment of the others.

MaryJo shakes her head at Erics comment, but Eric isn't baking down.

"Hey there's a lot of things I don't know about all of you. It's part of being a regular at the Pub. The past doesn't matter as much as the simple pleasure of good conversation over a couple of good drinks. Hell, I just ran into your husband a couple weeks ago for the first time and we've been arguing politics for a couple years now. It's nothing to feel all guilty about."

MaryJo turns to Elizabeth, "In spite of Erics comments, I for one am sorry I never knew about Johnny's daughter. I'm so glad you came by."

"Oh don't worry about it. I think Eric's right. I'd ask dad about the people he meets at the Pub and pretty much get the same response. Good people, good conversation. That's about it."

As Sue delivers the Tom Collins to Elizabeth, she joins the conversation. "So do you live around here?"

"Oh no, I am a doctor for Doctors Without Borders. That's probably one reason he didn't want to talk much about his personal life. Every time I called him he'd get all frustrated, ' I thought you were in the Middle East somewhere,' he'd say, 'No Pops, that was last month. They needed me in Africa, so I'm here now.' He would always get a good laugh at not being able to keep up with my travels. I'm quite certain that's why he was more than happy that none of you asked him about family. He'd probably get frustrated trying to explain what I do."

Elizabeth notices the Santa hat stuffed in her purse and perks up, "By the way, one of the reasons I wanted to come meet you all was to give you my dads Santa hat. I'm sure he'd be happy if you all kept it to remember him by." as she puts the hat on the bar.

Sue picks it up the hat with a reflective smile, "Are you sure, Elizabeth. Seems like this would be a good item for you to have in your travels?"

Elizabeth laughs, "No. He talked a lot about his role as Santa and how you all pitched in to help him with the kids. You guys should keep it. Besides, I have a house full of mementoes to go through that I have no idea what to do with. I have a condo just outside of New York City and probably spend about a month there through the year. I love being out in the field and have very little needs, so I'm going to sell the house and give away or sell everything in it and donate the money to Doctors Without Boarders, as dad requested in his will. If any of you want to come by and help me out by taking some of his stuff, you are welcome to it."

MaryJo of course, explodes with enthusiasm, "What about doing an estate sale and sell everything Johnny had and put it into a special account to help the kids and their families out at Christmas?"

Eric cuts her off, "MaryJo, Elizabeth just said all the proceeds go to Doctors Without Borders. And you accuse me of not listening. "

Elizabeth quickly responds, "Actually, that would be a great idea because the will says all the money should go to Doctors Without Borders or any other charity to his daughter's – that would be me – discretion. I would love to know that his work with the kids continues on."

MaryJo perks up again, "I think we could get his mailman friend Pete to help us out and do whatever we can to help families out all year long!"

"Hold on lefty! You make it sound like we'll have a fortune to spend on families. Johnny lived a pretty simple life and I'm guessing there won't be a whole lot of money from his estate," turns to Elizabeth, "No disrespect for your dad, of course."

"I have to say …. Eric, is it?" Eric nods , "This time you are wrong. My dad raised me to always be satisfied with enough." Everyone laughs in understanding how Johnny always talked to them that way too, "That's why I can work with Doctors Without Borders because of the way I was raised. I didn't want to be a doctor because of the money I could make, I wanted to be a doctor because of what I could do for those so desperate in need of medical care. My dad lived by example. His house is a simple house, his possessions are ENOUGH for an old man living alone. But he had a very successful career as an engineer and I can assure you that once I sell the house, all his possessions and close out his bank accounts, there will be more than enough for you all to create a foundation in his honor to help families in need. I think dad would love that."

Everyone is excited at the prospect of honoring Johnny as Sue refreshes many drinks behind the bar. She has laid down the Santa hat next to the flowers at Johnny's seat.

Elizabeth puts her drink down and continues the conversation, "You know, I'm out in the field a lot and you all know my dad is not one to talk much about his world. I was hoping to come here tonight to hear stories about my dad."

Surprisingly, Richard, the quiet one at the other end of the bar, is the first to speak up. "I saw Johnny a couple weeks ago at the grocery store. I didn't think much about it. Figured he wouldn't recognize me, you know. But as soon as he saw me, he perked up, 'Richard' he said, and he stopped and talked to me for a good five minutes or so. Asked how my family was doing and that he was sorry to hear about my moms passing. When I left the store, I thought what an incredible guy he was. I've always been a quiet type of guy and am always impressed with people like Johnny who can be so open and friendly to others. I know it's not that big a deal that Johnny stopped and talked to me, but it really impressed me."

Eric raises his glass, "To Richard… the quiet one."

"TO RICHARD!" the bar salutes as Richard's face turns a bit red from the attention.

This starts an evening of stories about Johnny. Many tears watering down the drinks on the bar and people making toasts. Hugs became the norm on this evening as Elizabeth embraced every story about her dad with no attempt to attend to the tears streaming down her cheeks. This was a special night for her, but not a surprise, as she grew up with a dad that was being reflected in every story she was hearing. This was truly a celebration of a great life.

As the stories begin to wind down, Elizabeth starts to gather her things to leave and asks Sue for her tab. This is greeted by a chorus of voices that makes clear that she will not be paying any tab on this evening. Elizabeth concedes.

"I'm so glad I came by tonight. I'm not surprised at how the evening went. My dad was a good man and I will miss him dearly as I do my mom. But mostly I will always appreciate that because of my dad, I have been able to share this evening with you all. Thanks for sharing your stories with me."

As she gets up to leave, Kim comes over to offer a hug. "If you're going to be around for a bit, I'd love to talk to you about your work. I just got my nursing license and my goal has always been to travel the world and use my nursing skills for the needy. I'd love your advice."

Elizabeth smiles, "Part of coming back to the states other than taking care of my dads estate, is to talk to young medical students and try to recruit more help. I would love to talk to you while I'm here, but be careful. If you're the one my dad talked about, I may be stealing you to go back to Africa with me." With that, Kim embraces Elizabeth in a smothering hug and lets Elizabeth know she would love that.

As Elizabeth leaves, Sue turns her attention to Johnny's seat.

"What do you guys think. I'm thinking of putting a plaque at the end of the bar that says, 'Santa's Seat. In loving memory of Johnny" and every night when I start my shift, I'll start by placing a Tom Collins at the end of the bar." as she did tonight.

Everyone approves the idea with a salute, "To Santa's Seat"

"What should we do with the hat?" asks MaryJo.

Kim chimes in, "How about we put it on the wall above the servers station and since Johnny was always telling us to only pursue enough, we can start a tradition that every time a server gets enough on a tip, they kiss their hand and tap the hat as a thank you to Johnny."

MaryJo perks up, "We could put a little Christmas bell on the hat so we will all know that every time a server kisses the hat, they have received enough from another customer. That would be such a nice way to remember Johnny."

Everyone raises their glasses in agreement, as Richard jumps in.

"Maybe we could have a cookout once or twice a year to raise money for the Johnny Foundation. Not sure how much money Elizabeth was talking about, but we'll need to have some way to add to it or it will eventually will run out."

"Are you any good at cooking on a grill?" asks MaryJo

Richard takes a sip from his beer, "Well I am the head cook at Bobby's Bar-B-Que, so I think I could do it."

Eric spits out his drink, "NO WAY!!!! I've gone to Bobby's a thousand times why haven't I ever seen you there."

"Well I'm the head cook. I don't need to see the people out front. I get there at 6am every day and start preparing all the meat that's been smoking over night. By the time the lunch crowd starts showing up, I'm busy prepping meat in the smoker for the next days crowd."

"Oh My God, that place has the best Bar-B-Que! You'd be able to do that here?"

"Well I wouldn't want to lose my job, but it's for a good cause and I'm sure the owner would be happy to have me help out. He's right down the street and he might even want to help out too."

Sue is busy replacing empty glasses with full ones as she joins in, "Does anyone know how to set up a foundation legally?"

Eric is almost insulted, "Are you kidding, I'm a lawyer ya know. I don't chase ambulances, I work in corporate law. I'd be happy to do all the work on my own time to set up the Johnny Foundation. I'll take care of that."

Maryjo can't resist and jumps in, "Sue did say legally, Eric. Do you think you can handle that?"

Eric laughs, "Oh MaryJo, you have to understand what legally is before you do something illegally you know. I'll make an exception for Johnny in this case and keep it spotless clean for you."

MaryJo raises her glass to Eric who responds in kind as the rest of the bar settles into their routine.

Later that night as Sue and Kim shut down the bar for the evening as the remaining few leave the premise. Kim picks up the Santa hat and Sue pours one final shot for the two of them.

"So Johnny had a daughter. Nobody saw that coming." says Kim.

"I know. It's funny, and yet sad. I learned more about my grandfather after he died. While he was alive, he was always just the old man who made me laugh. I guess we all do it. Johnny was the old man at the end of the bar that we loved. Then he dies and we find out he was a highly respected engineer who had a daughter who is a doctor saving lives all over the world. You feel guilty a little that you never really got to know these old folks, but then again, I think there's a lot of truth with what Eric said too. Hell, I didn't know Richard was the head cook at Bobbys! Who knew?"

Kim laughs, "I know, right. That quiet little guy at the end of the bar makes the best damn Bar-B-Que in the world and none of us had a clue. Crazy!"

Sue takes the Tom Collins from Johnny's seat and makes that the last glass she cleans as Kim turns out the lights and they both head for the door.

Kim pauses and looks back, "I guess my life will be

changing too, but I'll always have a deep appreciation for my time here at the Pub." she says as Sue puts her arm around her.

"We will miss you too, girl. But like the card you got at Christmas, if you ask for enough, you'll never want more. I'm thinking your time here was enough. It's time for you to go out there and save some broken lives."

"Rest in peace, Johnny" we hear as the door is locked secure.

PART II

The

Judgement

10

The GETA Foundation

One Forward Lane, Johnny reads the business card, then looks up at a very unimpressive building located out by the airport. These are small businesses that others would have to know about because they are not easily found. Not the kind of businesses that depend on any foot traffic, that's for sure. He checks the business card again. One Forward Lane, suite A. He looks up and sees the A above the door that simply says 'GETA' on it.

He's not sure if he should knock on the door or just go in, but being a business, he figures he could just go in, so he opens the door with a fair degree of hesitancy. Inside, he finds a rather large room that probably seems larger than it is because it is mostly empty. Just a desk with George sitting behind it, who responds to Johnny's arrival.

" Johnny! Glad you came by. Please come in." he says.

Johnny looks around and is frankly not very impressed. You'd think a non-profit would at least have pictures on the wall reflecting what they do . This place has nothing that Johnny can tell.

" So this is your foundation. Impressive." says Johnny trying to be polite.

George laughs, " Oh I know it's not impressive, but trust me Johnny, I'll explain it all to you and then it will begin to make more sense."

He offers Johnny a seat and then goes around the desk to his own chair.

"To begin, let me warn you that a lot of what I say today will make no sense to you, but if you just stay with me, I'll explain it all and it will make more sense as we go. You're welcome to ask any question along the way, in fact I encourage it."

He pauses to let Johnny soak it all in, well aware that at this point there's nothing to soak in but a large empty room with no pictures.

"Johnny, you passed away last night as you were reading your book and you are here because I'm not actually George Geta, I'm really an angel in charge of daily operations here on Earth and I wanted to offer you another option before you started your eternity."

"Excuse me?" says Johnny, not sure if he's talking to an angel, a lunatic or just having a bad dream.

"Yes, I know it's a bit much to take in, but I always find it easier to just lay it out there right away and then carefully walk you through the whole process."

Johnny looks down at his hands, then up at George as if to be working hard to make sense of it all.

"So I'm dead, and instead of any funeral, I just pop in here to hear about another option instead of eternity?"

"Yes. Well there was a funeral, a very nice one actually. I could show you if you'd like."

As he turns his small monitor around, Johnny starts to say something but stops.

"Elizabeth?" he says as he looks at the monitor and sees a scene of his daughter standing around what appears to be a chapel and she's talking with Sue and Kim from the Pub. He sits back in his seat confused.

"If I died last night, how could this be real?" he says as he points to the scene on the monitor.

"Well you have to understand that time on this side is much different than it is on earth. When I say you died last night, I was being literal. Your last night on earth was when you died, obviously. But time on earth keeps moving. Your daughter had to fly in from Africa and take care of your estate and while she was there, she went to the Pub and met all the wonderful people you knew there and it's all become a very nice time of celebrating your life and what you meant to them. But on this side, time has no value so it is whatever we make it to be." he pauses again to let Johnny soak it all in.

Johnny continues to stay glued to the monitor as he watches the funeral with mixed emotions. After an uncomfortable pause, he turns back to George and says, "Does Joe know you're an angel?"

George hesitates and takes a deep breath, "Actually, Joe is my boss. Joe is God." he says as he sits back and braces himself.

Johnny glares at George in confused contemplation. "Joe is really God… the almighty?"

"Well yes, he's God the creator. And whenever he comes here to help me recruit, he likes to create different personas just for fun. God loves to create different personalities."

"I see. So God has multiple personalities, you're saying?" Johnny asks.

George isn't comfortable with where this is going, "Listen Johnny, I know it sounds a bit crazy, but believe me, I will not let you leave here until you fully understand what this is all about." he says nervously.

"Well then, it's a good thing time has no value on this side, because you're not getting off to a good start." Johnny says as he sits back anticipating a long stay.

"I know, but really Johnny, it's not that complicated, either. God is the creator of everything, but from time to time, God likes to take a break and drop in and help me out. I could easily use other angels to recruit for me, but sometimes God enjoys coming and spending some time on this planet to see how the people are doing. God thinks it's good to drop in on all his planets from time to time and see how life is progressing. It makes sense, really. When he comes to this planet, he likes to become different roles depending on what I'm trying to recruit. So in this case, he decided to be Joe, a writer who is always doing research." He pauses to let Johnny think about it.

"So there is no Joe the writer and that's why he never answered any questions about his personal life?" Johnny says with a slight hint of understanding.

"Well he is God after all. You wouldn't want God telling lies really. That's why he almost always says he's a writer doing research. He's not telling you a lie."

Johnny is working his understanding, "So you're saying that God took a break from creating all the stars, suns, planets and everything else out there so he could come to this small little planet and become Joe, a writer doing research who hangs out with an old man at the local Pub just so he could recruit me? I can't wait to hear what exactly I'm being recruited for."

"Well God can take any number of assignments, but he chose yours because your time was drawing near it's finish and he really loved how you approached life with your message of enough for the kids when you were Santa. It's one of Gods biggest pet peeves. People are always asking him for more, more, more. He loves to find people who can give a message that if they focus on having enough, they'll never want more – one of the hardest messages for you humans to learn. But God loves how you actually got it and he really wanted to support you and see if you might be interested in spending some time helping him spread that message. He even gave me my name, George Geta and said my 'foundation' would stand for Giving Enough To All. He was very proud of that idea"

As Johnny contemplates this information, George sits back, appreciating the fact that Johnny came with a very low key emotional make up which is going to make his job much easier. The high strung people with compassionate hearts are always a tough assignment to work with.

"So Joe – or God – wants me to give up eternity and become a traveling salesman or evangelist or something?" questions Johnny.

George quickly replies, "Oh no, Johnny , you're not giving up your eternity. It will always be there and you will be able to start your eternity at any time . This is just a program we like to offer those who have a unique understanding of how God designed this planet and the people who live on it . You happen to have a firm understanding that the path to happiness is in pursuing enough, not more. It's a very valuable gift that few people understand. Of course we want to offer you the opportunity to stay here on Earth for a little bit and help us get that message to those in need."

George stops to give Johnny ample time to process the information and ask any questions.

"Do other people do this sort of work after they die?" asks Johnny.

"Actually, I have many ambassadors working on Earth. People with specific talents that can further other people's understanding of God . You would be good as an Enough Ambassador, but we have many other types of ambassadors working the Earth. Some do it for a little bit then want to move on, while others really connect and decide to make this their eternity. It's always up to the individuals to make it whatever they want it to be."

"Where would I go?" Johnny asks with a healthy dose of uncertainty, not sure if he's buying into this or not.

"I'll give you assignments. You'll be able to choose whichever one you want to work, then we'll come up with a plan that you are comfortable with and I'll make sure you have everything you need to complete the assignment. When you are done, we'll get together and review it and look at any other assignments you may be interested in."

Johnny hesitates in thought. "So you give me an assignment and I go out there and do what I can with it and when I'm done, I come back here to get another one?"

"Well you wouldn't come back here to this address. This was just set up for you and I to meet. If you take an assignment, we'll plan it all out including locations to meet for updates as well as a place for more in-depth talking if need be."

"And I'll be working in real time with people who are still living, but I will not be living?" Johnny asks.

"Yes, you'll be living just like Joe when he was recruiting you."

"So how did Joe live while he was recruiting me? Did he stay at a hotel or something when he wasn't at the Pub?" Johnny asks, always curious about what Joe did when he wasn't at the Pub.

George hesitates, "Well to be honest, Johnny, Joe is a bad example because, well, he is God. He really loves to take advantage of his time here on Earth and take in some of his favorite creations. He really loves some of the natural parks in this world. So whenever Joe was not at the Pub, he could be just about anywhere on the planet enjoying some sights and sounds that makes this planet unique. You'll be able to do that after you move on to your eternity, but you won't be able to do that while you're working with us. While you're working with us, you'll be staying at a hotel of your choosing. But remember, time has no value with you, so every time you wake up, you'll be working on your assignment."

Johnny thinks about it and is clearly not too sold on the idea yet, "How do you know when the assignment has had enough?"

"Think about the holidays you had. A lot of lives were touched just because Joe left $142 dollar tip. Once people got the message of asking for enough and not more, it pretty much takes on a life of it's own. And to be honest, it doesn't always turn out well. Joe got everyone started during a holiday of giving and that was great, but we may need another ambassador later on to go back to readjust someone's approach. It's a very fluid existence people have here on Earth. You see people all the time get very excited about something that is good and pure, but it doesn't take much for them to get discouraged or lose sight of the path they were headed. God understood that by giving humans a free will in such a diverse world, it was going to have many bumps in the road, so to say. That's why he made me head of Earth Operations and makes sure my ambassadorship program has enough people to work the planet."

George takes a break to let Johnny process what he is saying.

"I look at my ambassadors as farmers. They plant seeds in the open hearts and work with them until they can see the roots taking hold and a vine of hope begins to rise in their spirit. We don't always bare fruit, but we always plant the seeds and keep working the soil in their heart with the hope that some day it will."

Johnny thinks about all he has heard. It seems like an interesting system God has designed, and after the experience of the holidays, Johnny can see how it may be a nice thing to participate in, but he's still not 100% convinced.

"If I go to my eternity now, could I come back at any time and help out later?' Johnny asks to see what his options really are.

"Of course you can." George says, "But you must understand that we recruit people to help with our Earth programs before they receive their eternity because the reality is that only a few who start their eternity ever want to come back and help us out."

"So eternity must be pretty good, you're saying."

George smiles, "God is the ultimate creator and it is eternity. That is all I will tell you because if I told you what your eternity was, I'd have no chance of getting you into our Earth Operations program, that's for sure."

Johnny smiles with a hint of excitement, before refocusing on the program being discussed.

"Can you give me a couple examples I can look at before I decide what I want to do?"

George jumps up and heads to a file cabinet and pulls out a couple files that seem so outdated from the world as it is and hands them to Johnny as he is talking.

"Of course. We have two types of accounts in the Enough program. The first are those who for the most part come from a wealthy background or were spoiled when they were growing up. They are the ones that always want more and come from a heart of selfish greed. I don't see you working in that area, but we do have others who are excellent in providing the much needed humble pie to get these people rethinking their priorities. The second type are those who have come from a rough background of struggle who are always playing catch up with their finances and never seem to see any hope. Those are the accounts I think you would be great for. But of course, you are welcome to review any case and accept any one to your liking."

As he turns the monitor around so Johnny can see it, he pushes a button and pulls up an account, furthering the oddity of why there would be an outdated file cabinet in the first place.

For the next ten minutes or so, George and Johnny watch what Johnny considers a pretty good tutorial of some cases within the Enough Program featuring different strategies and approaches depending on the given situations.

Johnny's curiosity compels him to ask George as he hands back the old files full of papers, "In less than ten minutes, this video has given me full understanding of what your program does. I'm a bit confused on what these files you gave me are for?"

George doesn't hesitate, "Well young people of this world love quick answers and short videos to explain everything to them, but older folks like you typically value and appreciate the time spent going through actual files and studying the different reports, graphs and studies of a case before you decide what you want to do with it. So I like to have that process available for you, just in case."

Johnny smiles as he shakes his head, "Well I'm sure in your world where time has no value, there may be something to it, but for me, I appreciate the videos that simply give me the basic information and lets me go from there."

George returns the files back to their cabinet, and as he shuts the drawer, the cabinet disappears.

"No problem Johnny. We want to provide whatever our recruits are most comfortable with, so if the video instructions work well for you, we can simply stay with that."

As he takes his seat again, George continues, "Of course those were two examples of the many cases we have in this area." He hesitates with a hint of futility, "Unfortunately, there are a lot of people who have a dire need to learn the lesson of Enough. My job would be to match you with cases I feel would be best for your heart. Every recruit is different, so it's important to match my recruits with the cases that have the best opportunity for a recruit to succeed. That's the point of the program, of course."

"Of course," says Johnny, "So if I was to take an assignment, what exactly would I do?"

"Well you and I would review the case until you're completely comfortable with how the individual got to the point in their life that requires your help." He says as he looks to Johnny for any signs of confusion, then continues, "Then we would go over the different strategies that we could use that would help our client most until we both settle on one specific plan and make sure you have everything you need to be successful before you get involved."

Johnny hesitates, "And then I just show up in their life and do my thing?"

George smiles, "Yes. But remember, it's only after I am sure you have everything you need. As we discuss the case, we would decide what role would be best for you. Your spirit from your life on Earth – everything that you have learned that brought you to this point – will always be the same, but we may decide that you need to be a much younger you in a case. We may decide that you should be a great Doctor, or maybe a quiet homeless person. It doesn't matter, we can make your physical appearance be whatever we need it to be to get you into the best situation to help our client."

Johnny considers all this before asking another question. "How will I know I'm done?"

George smiles, "Oh trust me Johnny. There are many things I cannot give you until you are fully incorporated into your own eternity, but there are some things we can provide while you are working our program here that will serve to enhance your abilities in a positive direction. One of them is the ability to read other peoples eyes. The old saying you people on Earth have, "The eyes don't lie" is cute, but you really only scratch the surface of what information can be obtained from looking into other peoples eyes. If you take an assignment, you will have that moment when you say something, or your client will say something and you'll see clearly in their eyes that you've done enough and it's time to move on. It happened for Joe when he looked at Kim's eyes as she told him she was ordering steak with all the works for the young couple she was serving. He knew he had done enough and it was time to move on."

Johnny sits back and smiles in consideration as well as in reflection of his days at the Pub.

"So how's Joe doing?" he asks.

"Doing well. Some of the other planets get a little testy when he takes an assignment on this planet because he has so much fun checking out the many worlds you have created, but he enjoys his visits to all his creations and for the most part, all the angels understand that it's just God being God and there is no sense getting flustered about it. He'll do the same thing on their planet when he gets there and they know that. He is definitely a creator who fully takes advantage and enjoys everything he has created, that's for sure."

Johnny smiles and then asks, "Can I pop into the Pub sometimes? Maybe go by and see how things are going?"

George is quick to reply, "Oh no. The only rule is that you can not go home. I have plenty of assignments all over the world and you are welcome to request anywhere that you would like with the exception of your home turf. It's important for our recruits to stay focused on their clients and serve them. We just can't have our recruits working with clients they knew from their past life on Earth."

Johnny sits back with a look of understanding as he considers everything he is hearing. "What if we need to get together while I'm working an assignment? How do I get in touch with you?"

George smiles and delights at how Johnny seems interested in the program, "You will have an angel assigned to you that will be connected to your heart. Your assigned angel will always be available any time there is a question or situation that needs help. Because time has no value in our world we can pause whatever we are doing and get together with you whenever a situation comes up. While you and I have been talking here, for example, I've had to pause our conversation 243 times to get together with other recruits. For you it seems like we've just been casually sitting back and talking about my program, but in reality, I've been awfully busy coming and going during this time."

"So there will be an angel who can put my assignment on hold and tell me I'm screwing up and get me back on track?" Johnny asks a bit confused.

George laughs, "Not just when you are screwing up, but any time there is a need to communicate. The point is that you and the angel will always be connected to help with anything that comes up. We want you to succeed, not screw things up, of course."

"Seems like with the angels helping out like that, everyone who dies makes a good recruit." says Johnny in thought.

George seems uncomfortable at getting off the subject, "Of course. Everyone makes a good recruit. Now…."

Johnny interrupts, "Everyone? I'm guessing Charles Manson wasn't much of a recruit."

Georges shoulders drop in frustration, "Johnny, please. I am unable to discuss any other persons destiny with you, but of course some of my best recruits have come from death row. There are people who have done some horrible things in their life for sure. Created a lot of pain for others as well as themselves. After sitting on death row for many years waiting to be executed, you have time to reflect. Remember, God judges us by our hearts. There have been many horrible people who have been executed with pure hearts of love and remorse. They are so eager to have the opportunity to go back into the world and work with young people and steer them away from the things that got them in trouble. I get recruits from many environments and we use them as best we can to help others out. Now if we can return to your own recruitment, I think we are at a point of deciding what you would like to do."

He looks at Johnny with a big smile as Johnny considers his options.

"Well I wouldn't mind giving it a try, I suppose, as long as

I know if it doesn't work out I could always get started on my eternity."

George nods in agreement. "It's totally up to you, Johnny. I think you'd be an excellent recruit, but it's up to you and what you want to do."

Johnny sits back. "I'm sure there is a lot I don't understand about how this all works, but I'd be willing to give it a try. Where do I start?"

George smiles in victory.

11

The First Assignment

"So this is the one you want to start with?" asks George as he looks at the monitor.

Johnny sits back with uncertain confidence, "Yeah. She seems like a good kid who could really use some direction."

George doesn't need to review the case because he is an angel and knows all the cases by heart.

"Yes, she would be an excellent case to start with. So what would be your approach to helping her out?"

"Well she seems so discouraged with her injury and how she'll never be normal again. She seems like the kind of patient that will be looking for improvements by leaps and bounds, when in reality, she needs to approach it step by step."

George is excited, "You are absolutely right, Johnny. Sarah is a very ambitious and talented young lady who before the accident had so much to look forward to. The head injury she got on her skiing trip really set her back. It's going to take time for her to regain many of her skills, but it's a critical time for her to learn the message of enough. Not only in her physical recovery, but in her life. Her family structure is very ambitious. The whole family will need to learn the art of enough, but if you can get them to that level, they will all succeed and become the productive, positive people they were created to be."

Johnny hesitates, "So I have to work with the whole family? I thought I was just going to work with the girl?"

"That's the exciting part of the program, Johnny. You will be working with the girl of course, but in doing so, you can plant the seeds of enough to everyone around her. You have no idea what person or persons will connect with that seed of enough and become your greatest allies in your work. It may be her father, maybe her mother, maybe a nurse or a janitor. It doesn't matter. The point is to plant the seeds to everyone involved and trust that the message will take hold in someone's heart. The adventure comes in understanding that you are merely the messenger and the more hearts you can touch with that message, the more potential you'll have of seeing the fruits of your labor."

Johnny sits back, a bit overwhelmed, "Maybe I should start with a case that's a little easier. This one might be a bit too much for my first one."

George is quick to disagree, "This one is perfect for you Johnny. You'll be great. You just have to adjust your mind set a little. First you have to look at the worst case scenario. You could totally screw this assignment up and we would abort the whole thing, pat you on the back and tell you to go have a nice eternity, which, as I have already told you, is yours to enjoy, will never change and is awesome. That's the worst that could happen. Second, you will have an angel assigned to you that will accompany you in your first assignment. Your angel may be a nurse, or a patron of a bar, or a roommate at the hotel you are staying at. We can decide all that before you get started. Your angel will be available for any support you may need and give you advice for any situations that stump you along the way. You are not in this alone, Johnny. I have complete faith in your abilities and am confident that once you give it a try, you're going to really embrace the opportunities you have working in our program."

"If I'm going to have an angel with me, why do you need me? Why not have your angels do the work and let me go to my eternity?" Johnny asks.

"Oh Johnny, angels are totally different. They were created by God to simply work as his helpers. They are only spirits who can adapt to any environment on any planet to help with any given situation. Gods army, I like to call them. You'll have an angel to support your work, but the angel will not be seen by anyone and only heard by you, unless the situations calls differently. You are a human who understands human behaviors, so you – and people like you – are needed to help us here on earth."

Johnny pauses to take it all in. He's not completely sold on the project, but has a feeling that if he just gives it a shot, he'll come to realize the value this program has.

"So I would be living just as I did when I was alive? Eat meals just as I did, live and breath within the community where the hospital is and be able to walk around and experience the different aspects of the city, go to a ball game if I choose, whether it involves my work or not?"

"Of course, Johnny. Your work is to spread the message of enough. You can explore every opportunity you wish while you are there because every adventure you take may come with the opportunity for you to plant the seeds of enough. Sarah will be your main assignment, of course, but you may have several other opportunities to sow the seeds to others. I encourage everyone in my program to get out and explore their environments and look for opportunities beyond their assignments. There's a chance you may get nowhere with Sarah, but by exploring the community around the hospital, you may ignite others to the idea of seeking enough, not more, which would make the assignment absolutely worth the effort. If you just focus on Sarah and then sit in your hotel every night watching ball games, there would be too much pressure on you to succeed with Sarah. The more you get out and explore your opportunities, the more likely you are to have success stories from your experiences."

"So how would I pay for all this?" Johnny asks.

George smiles, "Good question." he pulls out a credit card and hands it to Johnny, " We have our own GETA Foundation credit card. It will never be rejected as long as you only use it for enough . $142 dollar tip on four drinks seems a bit excessive, but given the circumstances, it was enough, so it was approved. If you try to give someone a million bucks because you feel sorry for them, that's not going to fly. We need a specific amount for a specific purpose. We know your heart though, and I have complete confidence that you'll be reasonable in everything you do."

He leans over as if he doesn't want anyone else in the empty office to hear, "To be honest, the only one we ever have a problem with is Joe. He has rather expensive tastes, and a heart of compassion like no other. But he is God after all, so I have to remind my angel bookkeepers to just keep their comments to themselves and approve the charges." George sits back as Johnny is humored at the thought of his expensive friend Joe.

"So that's why Joe always wanted specific amounts when we were helping out the families at Christmas." He says in reflection.

"Well it would have defeated the purpose of the message if Joe left $500 dollars when Sue only needed 142, right?" George says as Johnny nods in 'good point' reflection.

"Listen Johnny, I think it's a great assignment for you and as I have mentioned, you'll be assigned an angel who will be with you every step of the way. Why don't you give it a try?"

Johnny takes a deep breath of surrender, "I guess it wouldn't hurt to give it a try."

"Excellent. Let's set up our plan."

As they begin to brainstorm for the adventures with Sarah, Johnny becomes an official member of the GETA Foundation.

12

———

The First Day

First day of his first assignment, Johnny is a bit reserved but anxious to get started. He feels good about the plan he and George developed and is especially pleased to look in his hotel room mirror and see a much younger version of himself staring back – late 40s, maybe 50.

The plan calls for him to be a representative of the American Head Injury Association whose job it is to work with people with head injuries and to support their treatment and doctors by reviewing the treatment plan and encouraging the patient throughout the process.

As he walks down the hall of the hospital, the weight of his mission begins to take hold and Johnny begins to question why anyone would delay an awesome eternity – which he has no idea what it is other than awesome – to take on something like this. There is a hint of hope that this assignment fails miserably so he can say he gave it a shot and it didn't work out and he can just go to his awesome eternity and be left alone.

"Room 1304, well too late to turn back now." Johnny says as he knocks on the door. A soft 'Come in' encourages Johnny to open the door into a rather dark room, which makes sense given the injury. There is no one in the room but Sarah, which is good news for Johnny as he was hoping to start off his relationship in a quiet, one to one setting. Sarah is lying in her bed staring out the window with little concern for who it is walking into her room.

"You must be Sarah." Johnny says to break the silence.

Sarah turns and looks at Johnny with a look of apathy, "Gee, what gave it away?"

"Well there's no one else in the room and the bandage on your head pretty much indicated I was in the right place." Johnny says, not letting the sarcasm get to him.

The look of apathy on Sarah's face is not encouraging, "Well now we both know who I am, so who are you, another doctor to poke and prod my body and tell me everything is going to be great?"

Johnny smiles, "No Sarah, I'm not a doctor. I don't poke or prod anyone. My name is Johnny and I represent the American Head Injury Association."

Sarah looks at Johnny unimpressed, "Oooo, I qualify for a club full of head jobs? My lucky day" she says dripping with sarcasm.

Johnny learned a long time ago that when you are working

with negative, sarcastic people, you always stay on point and never let the negativity drag you down.

"Sarah, I'm here as a support for you and your family. To answer any questions you may have about your treatment. To make clear to you the limitations as well as the possibilities every step of the way."

"So you're my personal cheerleader who's going to make me feel great about my life being over?"

Johnny refuses to buy into her cynical attitude, "I don't have any pom poms, and if your life was over, it would be Gods responsibility to make you feel great about that, not me"

As he takes a seat, Sarah goes back to staring out her window.

"Listen Sarah, you had a pretty serious head injury and I didn't expect to come in here and find you all perky and bright. The road ahead is not going to be an easy one for sure, but at least you have a road ahead of you. And that road gives you the opportunity to establish your story as a winner or a loser. It's up to you. I came here because I read your history and I believe you to be a winner. I want to help you become the winner you have inside your heart. Or you can choose to be a loser and sit around in your pity-party and feel sorry for yourself. If you do, then you don't need me. I can go back and find another case that has potential." Johnny stops to let it all soak in. His tone is firm, but gentle and non-threatening.

Sarah appears numb with tears gathering in her eyes as she considers what Johnny has said.

"Well you're not a very good cheerleader." Sarah says in a softer tone.

Johnny smiles, "You're right about that, Sarah. A cheerleader would be cheering and getting all excited when the team is behind 40-0. I'd be over at the bench smacking the players upside the head with my pom-poms, telling them they suck and to get out there and give us something to cheer about!"

Sarah smiles. "So how do you plan to encourage me?" she asks.

"I'm not here to encourage you or discourage you, Sarah. I'm here to be honest in your approach to treatment so you can stay focused on what you need to do to get better. The encouragement or discouragement comes from your heart."

"So you're saying the doctors aren't honest and that's why I need you around to tell me the truth?" she says with a strong dose of apathy.

"Doctors talk in medical terms and focus on your injuries. I only focus on your heart. Attitude plays a big role in your ability to recover and how completely you recover. I'll be with you as long as it's needed to keep your recovery on track."

"So you're here to make me all perky and feel happy about having spotty memory of what happened in my past, or that my future may not include many of the things I loved to do a week ago?"

"Well Sarah, I'm not really going for the perky approach. You have a rough road ahead of you. There are going to be some tough valleys to travel in order for you to get to the top of the mountain again. Being perky is not going to get you through those valleys, being determined will."

"Well I'm sorry, mister cheerleader, but I'm not feeling very determined right now. You might want to go back and find someone else you can root for."

"Sarah, I get it how pissed off you are at the world right now. I understand the sarcasm dripping from every comment you make. I understand that you would rather crawl into a cave and be left alone than to constantly hear doctors, nurses and complete strangers tell you how everything is going to be great. I get that. Those feelings are no problem for now and don't bother me at all because I know you're going to need some of that pissed-off attitude to get through some of the valleys you face. I am more encouraged now than I was earlier because I have no doubt that you have that emotional presence to beat this thing. Your negative attitude is okay for now. It's only been four days. But I'm confident that if we can get that negative attitude channeled into a positive, focused determination of not letting this accident change who you are, you're going to blossom into the great person you were meant to be. I absolutely am encouraged about your future."

Sarah looks at Johnny, taking in everything he has said. "I'm just not feeling as optimistic as everyone else right now." she concedes.

"Of course you don't. You feel like someone took a baseball bat to the side of your head. You're having trouble remembering the events of your past. They have meds running through your body that helps everything but your heart. Your attitude sucks right now because your life sucks right now. That makes total sense to me. I'm here merely to let you know it's not a forever situation. It will get better. You will laugh again. You will be able to do the things you love again. But only when you decide to channel that negativity into a positive determination to get the hell out of this situation life has thrown at you. YOU control the attitude, Sarah, and your future is determined by the attitude you chose now."

Another knock on Sarah's door and a nurse walks in without waiting for a reply.

"Don't mind me, I'm just here to check the monitors and med levels and make sure you're comfortable. My name is Nurse Prescott, but most of my patients call me Pooh because I'm sweet as honey and I don't let any of my patients become Eeyore. Are you comfortable, Ms Sarah?" nurse Prescott asks as she looks over the monitors next to Sarah's bed.

"I'm fine." says Sarah who seems a bit preoccupied in thought.

"Well you two go ahead with what you were talking about, I won't be botherin' you none." Nurse Pooh says.

Johnny gets up to leave, "I think I'm done for now. Sarah, it was nice to meet you and talk with you. I just wanted to come by and introduce myself for now. Think about what I said. The road ahead is not going to be easy, I won't lie to you. But where the road leads you is up to you. You choose the destination through your attitude. I'll drop by tomorrow to see how you're doing."

Without a response from Sarah, Johnny leaves the room. Nurse Prescott, never the one to let a conversation die out, jumps right in where Johnny left off.

"I don't know who that fella is, but I'd listen to what he has to say, girl. He sounds like a man with a good heart who knows what he's talking about." she leans over to Sarah, "And there's so few men who can do that, ya know."

Sarah smiles, "It's just hard to think that things will ever get back to normal. It's going to take so long before I can do things again."

"Oh child, you need to pray! I saw your charts. You need to thank God that you're still alive. You need to thank God that the road ahead doesn't have wheelchair ramps on it. You need to pray for patience to pave that road towards a beautiful destination. You're gonna be fine, but that man was right. Only your attitude can choose the destination."

"I wish I had more patience. This is going to be hard." Sarah says as she stares out her window.

"Honey, you have enough patience. God always gives us enough of what we need to get through any obstacles in our life. But you have to ask for it and believe. That's the difference between winning and losing. You have to ask and believe. You've got this, girl."

As nurse Pooh washes her hands, Sarah looks a bit overwhelmed with what lies ahead.

"Can I get you anything sweetheart?" the nurse asks.

"No. I'm fine." Sarah says.

"Okay, girl. I'll be here all night, so if you need anything you just buzz me. Otherwise, I'll leave you be."

With that, nurse Pooh leaves Sarah alone with her thoughts.

Meanwhile, Johnny heads back to his hotel room feeling fairly good about his initial interaction with Sarah. He wasn't surprised by her negative attitude and was pleased that he was able to counter it with simple common sense and a pinch of humor. As he enters his room, he is startled to find a young man sitting in a chair, feet propped up on the bed, watching TV. He looks at the number on the door to make sure he's in the right room, then looks at the intruder.

"May I help you?" he asks.

"Hey," says the intruder, giving only a slight glance at Johnny but careful not to miss any of what appears to be a baseball game, "How ya doin'?"

Johnny seems a bit miffed, "Who are you and what are you doing in my room?" he asks.

"I'm Alex," he says, staying with the ball game, "I'm the angel that was assigned to hang with you on your first assignment." He looks to Johnny with a smile and hand extended for a shake without getting up.

Johnny disregards the hand gesture. "And this is how you're going to help me? Sitting in my room watching baseball?"

"Pretty much. I'm just here if you need me and so far, you seem to have everything under control." he pauses as he watches another play on the game, "I really enjoy baseball. That's why I enjoy these assignments." he turns his attention to Johnny who is standing there baffled, "Do you like baseball? I could change the channel if you wish." he says with an annoying smile.

"No. I mean, yes, baseball is fine. But you don't seem like much of an angel." Johnny says with a strong dose of confusion.

"Would you feel better if I had a white robe, wings and a halo? I can do that, but since you are the only one who can see or hear me, I like to go the more casual look if it's okay with you."

Johnny doesn't respond as he closes the door and sits on the end of the bed without losing his stare at Alex, who continues to watch the game. The game breaks to a commercial, so Alex mutes the TV and turns his attention to Johnny.

"You really got off to a good start with Sarah. I think you're going to have this assignment nailed in no time." he says with that annoying smile.

"You were there?" Johnny asks a bit confused as this is the first he has seen him.

"Nope. I'm not going to follow you around." he says as he turns to the TV with the remote and changes the channel. "You must be Sarah." "Gee, what gave it away?"

Johnny looks at the monitor, then to Alex who is watching Johnny with a big smile, as he quickly flips the channel back to the game.

"Angel technology is way better than humans. I don't

have to do anything but sit here and watch baseball and follow your moves without missing a thing. It's really a cool assignment." the angel says without missing a play.

"And how is that going to help me?"

"I'm not here to help you, I'm here to be available if anything comes up. Your first day went well. I think you hit it off great with Sarah. There's a good chance you may not ever need me and that's a good thing. Your assignment is to help Sarah, while mine is to be available to you if you need any help. You may not need any help, and that's great because it means I can watch a lot of baseball while you're doing your thing helping Sarah out." He smiles.

That smile is so annoying, yet Johnny begins to process the conversation and avoids making any judgement thoughts about the angel assigned to him.

"So you're going to just sit here and watch games while I come and go to work with Sarah?"

"Oh no. I have the room next to you. I'm an angel, so I don't need any food, sleep or anything like that. You're still a human. A dead human I suppose, but with the same characteristics as humans. You need to sleep, eat and all that stuff. So I'll go back to my room when we are done here and leave you be." again with that smile.

Johnny looks at Alex with a pained look, "How did you get to be an angel?"

Alex considers the inquiry, "Not sure, really. I know we have no Moms or Pops. And I know we don't come from human life forms. I think God just whips us up whenever he needs more angels, really."

"Are all the angels like you?" Johnny asks

"I'm not sure about that either. It's not like we have meet 'n greets or potluck dinners or anything. We just go from one assignment to another." he pauses in thought before continuing, " To be honest, I'm not sure if I've ever met another angel or not. But they're out there. I'm guessing God creates angels with different characteristics to serve different situations. He's quite a creative creator."

Johnny sits on the bed with his arms crossed, studying Alex, not sure what to make of his angel assistant while Alex smiles that annoying smile before breaking the standoff.

"Well Johnny, unless you have any questions about today, I'll head back to my room so you can get some rest. You did great today. I think you're going to be a fine ambassador for God." he smiles as he gets up, "You're a natural, Johnny boy. I'm thinking I'll get to watch a lot of baseball on this assignment."

After a brief pause for a response, Alex simply smiles and disappears as the TV goes off, leaving Johnny quietly sitting on his bed looking around in complete astonishment. He gets up and goes to the fridge to make himself a drink for a nightcap as he mumbles, "He didn't even use the door. He better not do that every time while I'm on assignment."

From the other side of the wall, Johnny hears, "Don't worry, Johnny boy. I'll always knock on the door first. Sleep well!"

With that, Johnny takes a healthy draw from his drink and sits in his chair to wind down.

13

—

The Parents

The next morning, Johnny can be found in the small coffee shop having a cup of coffee and reflecting on this new world of his. He's starting to realize some of the perks of being dead, yet alive. For instance, he sat down at his desk last night in his room to write down some notes from his visit with Sarah, as he was prone to forget details and always felt he had to write down notes every night in order to remember things. As he was thinking about the visit, he was amazed at how his memory recalled every little detail of his visit as if he had access to instant reply and could pull up any part of the conversation at will. He had this odd feeling of comfort in knowing this was part of his new world and not just a matter of being 45 years old instead of 85 when he was still alive. He also noticed that his senses were a lot clearer in his new world. His vision, hearing and ability to decipher situations around him were a lot keener, which made his new world a lot more fascinating.

When Johnny was alive, he would spend his mornings with a cup of coffee and the newspaper to catch up on all the latest news. But on this assignment, he didn't want to hide behind a newspaper, he wanted to observe his surroundings and feel the beat of the moment.

He notices a conversation going on in the booth behind him. Two women are discussing the financial struggles of being a single parent. It reminded him of the time Joe left the $142 dollar tip for Sue and he thought this might be a good opportunity to test the waters of his new credit card. He quietly listens to the girls talking, hoping to hear a specific amount that he could take ownership of, but the conversation never goes that way. He is frustrated, but then remembers how George always talked about sowing the seeds of 'enough', so he decides to simply pay for their breakfast, and see if that would do anything.

As his server comes to refill his coffee, he tells her of his plan to pay the tab of the girls behind him anonymously. She smiles big and winks at Johnny.

When the server walks away, a young man gets up from the booth in front of Johnny. It is Alex, his angel assistant. As he puts on his jacket, he smiles at Johnny. "Very smooth, Johnny boy …. very smooth. I think I'll go watch some baseball" and walks out of the coffee shop.

The server goes to the ladies behind Johnny and asks if there will be anything else.

"No thanks, we need to get going. If you can just bring us the bill." says one of them.

"There is no charge today, ladies." the server says with a big smile.

The girls look at each other, then at the server confused.

"Guess you ladies have a guardian angel looking out for you because your tab has already been paid. Have a nice day."

As the server walks away, the girls wonder who might have paid their tab.

"I bet it was that young hunk that just walked out of here."

They both giggle in excitement as Johnny bows his shaking head in disbelief. Then he raises his head with a confused look and thinks to himself, 'Hey, wait a minute, I thought I was the only one who could see Alex? Oh, we are so going to have to talk about that tonight, that's for sure."

****

Johnny gets to room 1304 and knocks on it. A different voice says 'come in', so Johnny cautiously opens the door to come in and notices an older couple with Sarah that Johnny assumes would be her parents.

"Sorry to interrupt. I could come back another time Sarah, if you'd like."

Sarah replies in her voice of apathy, "That's okay, it's just my parents. Mom, Dad, this is Johnny. He works with head jobs. He's my cheerleader of sorts."

Johnny is not overwhelmed by the introduction, but extends his hand to the father.

"Tom Bradley, good to meet you." the father says with a firm handshake.

Then to her mother. "Shirley. So are you a doctor, then?" she says with a very innocent, soft voice.

"No mam, I represent the American Head Injury Association. I'm here to follow her treatment and make sure she has everything she needs."

Mr Bradley jumps right in, "Well she won't need much from you, Johnny. This is one tough girl and I know she'll be hitting the slopes again before the season ends."

Mrs Bradley jumps in, "Oh Tom, please! Sarah is going to need time before she is able to take on such dangerous activities." as she holds Sarah's hand to her heart.

Mr Bradley snaps right back, "There ya go again, Shirley, coddling your daughter. She's a tough cookie. She just needs to get to work, shake the cobwebs out of her head and go back and show that mountain who's the boss. She'll be fine."

Johnny looks at Sarah who is looking at him with a broken smile of futility, as Johnny turns back to Tom.

"Well Mr Bradley…"

"Call me Tom."

"Okay ….. Tom …. I don't question Sarah's toughness, but she had a pretty serious head injury and it will take some time and hard work before she gets back to that mountain."

"Don't sell my baby girl short, Johnny. I've been hangin' around her since she was pooping in diapers and I'm just say'n only a fool would bet against her."

"I'm not betting against your daughter, I'm just saying that we deal with reality here and the reality is that she is going to need every ounce of that toughness and time to have any chance of getting back on that mountain. With head injuries like that, even if you told me she could walk on water, it would still take time to heal and get back to a life she knew before" Johnny says with a bit of an edge to his tone.

"Well hell Johnny, if she could walk on water, she wouldn't have tripped up on the mountain in the first place." Tom says with a chuckle, pleased at his sense of humor that apparently no one else sees.

Johnny looks at Sarah, who has her eyes closed, head down and shaking as Shirley lets go of her hand and turns her attention to Tom.

"Oh Tom, let's go before you make a complete fool of yourself." as she grabs Toms arm and turns to Johnny. "You'll have to forgive my husband, he's a little outspoken at times. We'll leave you and Sarah alone so you can talk."

With that Shirley drags Tom out of the room and the atmosphere becomes a much calmer situation. Johnny looks to Sarah, who raises her head and has a look of disgust as Johnny smiles.

"You want me to call the nurse for some meds? I'm sure your head is throbbing about now."

Sarah smiles at Johnny, "I'm sorry about my dad. He's not an easy pill to take. I'll be fine."

"Well the good news is that now I understand where you get your perkiness." Johnny says with a smile.

Sarah laughs, but quickly stops herself as laughing makes her head hurt.

"He means well, but he's a stubborn businessman who has

trouble listening to others. He was a big football player in college and always complains at the TV for how soft the players are today."

"I'm sure they're good parents, Sarah." Johnny says as Sarah looks to Johnny with tears in her eyes.

"You know, Johnny, I've never had one moment when I felt my dad looked at me as his daughter." she says with a strong sense of pain. " Do you have any kids?"

"I had a daughter." Johnny says.

"I'm sorry, did she pass away?" says Sarah with a sorrowful look.

Johnny quickly panics as he realizes his mistake and scrambles to recover.

"Oh no, I still have her, of course! I mean she's still alive and all. What a great girl, too."

Sarah smiles, "I guess you were a pretty good dad, right?"

Johnny smiles as he is happy to move on from his near catastrophe, "Well Sarah, I never played football. In fact I was asked not to come back on co-ed bowling nights in college. I'd have to say my testosterone was pretty much shot long before they put my little girl in my arms"

Sarah again laughs with pain. "Maybe I could use some meds if I'm going to talk to you much more." she says.

As Sarah pushes the call button, Johnny smiles as he realizes he is seeing a much different Sarah today than yesterday. She has a charming smile and her eyes can light up any young man's heart.

"Well since your dad has left, let's talk about you and how things are going for you."

Sarah looks back at Johnny, "I guess better. I know I wasn't very positive yesterday, but I thought a lot of what you and nurse Pooh said. It made me realize that I will feel better when I just accept the injury for what it is and focus on doing what I can to get well again."

"That's good. The key is to not look for leaps and bounds in your progress but step by step. The doctor tells me you are able to write, correct?"

Sarah nods hesitantly, "I think so. Haven't needed to since the accident, but I'm thinking I can."

"Good. I brought you a notepad and pens because I think it's very important for you now to keep a daily journal. Every night write your feelings down. Don't worry about being proper. Speak your mind. No one but you will ever read your journal – unless you want them to. If you're pissed off, write it. If you're frustrated, write it. If you had a good day, write it. It's your journal and it's only for your eyes. I always have my clients write in their journals because I know that three months from now, you're going to snap at me or someone else with your pissie attitude, complaining of how you're not getting anywhere. That's when I want you to go read page one, read page two. Sarah, people in your position are always looking for more, but I'm here to teach you to pursue enough. People who always want more will never be satisfied. They always want more. I want you to seek enough. Enough work every day to take another step.

Enough patience to take another step. Enough strength to take another step. Focus on having enough and I promise you that you'll find satisfaction every night when you lay your head down to rest. If you always seek more, you'll never go to bed satisfied."

There is a knock on the door as nurse Prescott walks in with a glass of water and meds.

"Ms Sarah, is this man giving you a headache, girl?"

Sarah smiles, "No. That would be my dad."

Pooh turns to Johnny, "You're Mr Bailey? Nice to meet you, I'm nurse Prescott, but you can call me Pooh."

Sarah laughs, "No, no, no …. not him … my dad is what gave me the headache. This is Johnny. He's with the American Head Job Association."

Pooh looks over at Johnny who smiles, "It's actually called the American Head Injury Association. She's getting closer."

Pooh laughs, "Oh yes, I've read notes about your organization" She looks to Sarah, "You listen to this man, you hear. Those are good people who help a lot of others in your situation, so mind what he says."

She looks at the monitors and asks Sarah in a much more serious tone, "Where did you get your headache? I know it was from your dad, but was it stress? Was he stressing you out, 'cause I can talk to him, you know. I want my patients to only worry about their injuries and getting well. I don't care if he is your father, I'll run anyone out of this hospital who puts undo stress on any of my patients."

Sarah jumps in, "No. I was laughing."

Pooh steps back from the monitors, "Laughing? Your dad makes you laugh? Girl, I apologize for speaking ill of your father like that"

Sarah jumps in again, "No, Pooh. My dad didn't make me laugh, it was Johnny after my dad left that made me laugh."

"Well girl, now you're giving me a headache. Take your medication before I take it myself , and remember, who ever is making you laugh is always welcome here, but if anyone is stress'n you out, you let Pooh know and I'll ban them from the hospital in a heartbeat, ya hear."

As Sarah hands Pooh the glass, she responds, "Yes Pooh. My dad isn't easy to love, but I've been around him all my life and am use to him treating me like a teammate on his football team and not like a daughter. He is what he is and he's too stubborn to think that he'll ever change."

"Well you just remember that nurse Pooh is on your side. I've dealt with a lot of men like your dad and I have no problem in reminding him you're his daughter. Girl, that's why God created Eve. Everybody knows it was Adam who told her to go get him that apple. And just like a man, he blamed her when they got busted for it too. I'll check on you later." she says as she opens the door to leave.

Johnny looks over to Sarah, "I like that nurse." he says with a broad smile.

Sarah smiles too, "Yeah, between the two of you and my dad, I suppose, I'm thinking I'm not going to get a lot of sympathy around here."

"Well you'll get the sympathy from nurse Pooh and I, but

you won't get any pity. As for your dad, I can only say there is always hope. You just have to remember the positive support you have around you and trust that support to work for your benefit."

"Well my dad means well, but these last couple days I've come to understand that what you and Pooh say is a lot more accurate than what my dad says. I can feel in my body that this is not going to be an easy fix."

"Well you just have to keep in mind that everyone is different. Understand that doctors really can't tell you when you'll be able to do the things you want to do because people respond differently to treatment. Some recover rather quickly and some never do. A lot of it truly does depend on your attitude and determination. And to be honest, that may be something you can thank your dad for. A little spiritual kick in the butt to get back on that horse is not completely a bad thing. It may well be your mother who becomes the bigger problem. Skiing isn't nearly the dangerous activity she suggested and you might want to be aware of her over protective reach as well."

Sarah smiles, "So you're saying both my parents are screwed up." she says matter-of-factly.

Johnny smiles in frustration, "Well I'm trying to be positive here, but the absolute point is – regardless of your parents – it's all about you and the attitude you bring to your treatment. All the charts, parents and case histories can contribute, but the bottom line is that it's up to you. Your attitude, your ability to stay focused on the reality of the moment, and the determination in your heart to do enough every day to keep taking those baby steps that will eventually get you where you want to be. The people who do not succeed are the ones who always want more and get frustrated and give up. You have to have the mind set of 'I need to do enough today to take another step forward?"

Johnny can see the medications kicking in, and gets up to leave. "I'll let you rest, Sarah. I think you're going to do great. Just remember not to get sucked into the 'more' attitude. Make a goal each day and do enough to make that next step happen. I'll check back with you soon."

"Thanks, Johnny. I do appreciate you being here."

"Happy to help." says Johnny as he exits the room.

As he approaches the nurses station, he sees nurse Prescott alone and decides to stop and touch bases with her. She may be a big help to Johnny's mission.

"So nurse Prescott."

"Oh please, Johnny, just call me Pooh. I love being called Pooh, really, because it reminds everyone how sweet I am." she says with an engaging smile.

"Okay … Pooh … so you haven't met Sarah's parents yet?"

"No, not yet. I mostly work nights, so I don't always meet the family members."

"Well after meeting you, I'm thinking you might be a good connection for me as I work with Sarah."

"Are the parents an issue for Sarah?"

"Well they could be. Mr. Bailey appears to be a supportive fatherly type, but he's not very realistic. He comes from a football mentality of get up, shake it off and get back on that mountain again and show them who's boss. I tried to explain to him the severity of her injuries, but it was pretty clear that he fully expects Sarah to get back on that mountain and ski again before the season is over."

Pooh shakes her head, "That poor child. She's going to need a lot of patience to get back on that mountain."

"I know. I'm trying to teach her to focus on baby steps and to avoid the trap of always wanting to do more. People who constantly want more will never have enough and never be satisfied which doesn't create a positive attitude, which is so important for her recovery. After meeting her father, I'm guessing he's not going to be much help."

Pooh shakes her head in agreement, "What's her mother like?"

"She's on the other end. Very protective type. She doesn't want to even talk about her daughter getting back on that dangerous mountain."

Pooh shakes her head again, "And we have poor Sarah in the middle of all this. That poor child."

"I know. It's not hopeless. It's not the first time we've seen this kind of dynamics in families, but it is important that those of us working with Sarah are on the same page. I've always felt that when people always ask for more, they never have enough, but if they always ask for enough, they'll never need more. I think in Sarah's situation, that's going to be important for her recovery."

"I couldn't agree with you more, Johnny. I'm glad you

filled me in on her parents. You can count on me to give Sarah an ear full every night I'm here, that's for sure. And her parents too, if I run into them."

"I appreciate it, Pooh. I'll let you get back to your work. I just wanted to give you my take on it all."

As Johnny starts to walk away, Pooh shouts out, "You are heaven sent, Mr Johnny … heaven sent."

Johnny looks back and smiles, "Indeed I am, Ms Pooh… Indeed."

****

As Johnny opens the door to his room, he once again finds Alex relaxing with his feet propped up on the bed watching another baseball game.

"Hey Johnny boy, welcome home. You did some pretty nice work with Sarah today. I'm going to get a lot of baseball games in on this assignment, that's for sure."

As Johnny hangs up his jacket, he is anxious to cut to the quick, "Never mind my work with Sarah, I want to know what happened this morning at the coffee shop."

Alex mutes the TV and looks at Johnny a bit confused, "What do you mean?"

"After you left and the server told the girls behind me that their bill was paid by some guardian angel, they both said it must have been you."

Alex smiles, "I think they specifically referred to me as 'That Hunk'." he says with a healthy dose of pride.

Johnny is quick to reply, "I thought nobody else could see you and here these girls are giving credit to 'That Hunk' for paying a bill that I paid." he says with a noticeable edge in his tone.

"Well Johnny boy, the whole idea of seeing me or not seeing me is strictly an option. There are many situations where it's beneficial for me to be seen and heard only by you. But there are other situations where being seen and heard by others is a good thing. It's all about doing whatever is necessary to get people connected to God."

"How is being seen as 'that hunk' beneficial to anyone but you this morning?" Johnny asks with a bit of sarcasm.

"Johnny, Johnny, Johnny … you have to understand that angels don't have egos. Though to be honest, that was pretty cool when they called me a hunk, I admit, even though I'm not sure exactly what a hunk is, but it sounded like a pretty sweet thing by the tone they used. But you should really be thanking me for being seen this morning, not complaining about it."

Johnny is confused, "Thanking you? Why should I thank you for taking credit for something I did?"

Now Alex looks a bit confused, "Well you specifically told the server that you wanted to pay their bill anonymously, and it doesn't get much more anonymous than when someone else gets credit for it, don't you think?"

Johnny is left speechless and just stares at Alex, who has that annoying smile.

"Johnny boy, you're doing great. You helped those girls out by paying for their breakfast, you made good progress with Sarah and I'm thinking that nurse Pooh is going to be a great support for you on the inside. You're doing great so far, but I must warn you. You have to stay focused on the assignment. As your angel, I have to make sure you don't develop any kind of ego as you are helping others out, and I promise you I will be there to take the credit every time you help others in order that you don't get too smug about yourself. That's my job, Johnny boy, and you better get use to it." He smiles at Johnny who feels a bit smaller.

"I wasn't being smug."

"Oh Johnny boy, you come in here all pouty because you don't like me getting credit for something you did is a pretty strong statement of smugness if you ask me. The fact that this is your first assignment, I'm willing to let it go as a learning experience for you. But it's important that you understand the assignment and that everything we do is for the benefit of Gods work."

Johnny pauses in thought. What Alex is saying makes sense, of course, and for the first time, he looks at Alex as truly a support for him.

"Well I guess I still have a lot to learn. I'm sorry I snapped at you."

"You're doing great, Johnny boy. Don't say you're sorry, say thank you. Together we made those girls have a nice day. That's team work buddy boy and that's what we're here for."

Johnny looks at Alex in a conciliatory manner, "Well thank you Alex." as he pauses in thought, "So how do I know if you are being seen by everyone or not?" he asks.

Alex smiles, "Good question. Hey, how about we develop

a signal like they do in baseball? What if I do something like this (he goes through a massive array of signals) and if you see me do that, then you know I can be seen by others." he says with excitement for his plan.

"Hold on there, Angel boy. First of all, if you do that and everyone else in the coffee shop can see you, they are going to think you're crazy. And secondly, whatever we decide on has to be simple and subtle"

Alex looks a bit disappointed at how Johnny bursts his enthusiasm, but as he thinks about it has to admit he makes a good point. "Well I suppose we could come up with something a little more subtle. How about I wink at you and that means everyone can see me?"

"But how will I know you're giving me the signal or you have something in your eye?"

Alex looks at Johnny dumbfounded, "I'm an angel. I'm a spirit. If I wink at you, it's because I'm letting you know everyone can see me, not because I have something in my eyes. I don't have eyes, Johnny boy, I'm an angel."

Johnny is taken back a little, but the point is well taken. "Oh, right. So if you wink at me, I know everyone else around us can see you and we need to watch our conversation. Just make sure you do it first thing because I don't want to spend a lot of time watching people and trying to figure out if they can see you or not."

Alex gets up to leave, "Oh Johnny boy, we're a team. I'm working with you, not against you. If you see me in public and I wink first thing, that means everyone can see me and hear what we say. If I don't wink right away, it means don't talk to me because nobody sees me and will think you're an idiot talking to thin air. Either way, I will make sure you understand before anything unfortunate happens, I promise you that." Alex smiles at Johnny as he makes his way to the door and as he leaves, the TV turns off suddenly.

Johnny shakes his head in reflection as he walks over to the kitchenette to fix himself another strong nightcap.

14

——

The Day Off

When Johnny wakes up the next morning, he is startled to find Alex in the chair watching another game.

"How can there be a baseball game this early in the morning?"

"Oh Johnny boy, angel technology is so cool. I can watch all the baseball I want, any time I want." Alex says with that smile.

"And what are you doing here in my room, so early in the morning?" Johnny asks.

"I came to let you know you have the day off today." He says casually as he watches the game.

"Have the day off? What does that mean?"

Alex mutes the TV and turns his attention to Johnny, "That means no hospital today. You are free to get out and explore the town or do whatever you'd like. But no hospital."

Johnny looks concerned, "Is there something wrong with Sarah?"

"No, not outside her noggin, of course. Nurse Pooh is just going to have an encounter with Sarah's parents today, and it would be a really good idea for you not to be around there."

Johnny pauses and smiles, "I had a feeling that nurse Pooh would be a great support. Do you know what's going on?" he asks Alex.

"Nope. I just get a signal to keep you away from the hospital today. It could be a good thing or a bad thing. Guess you'll find out later." he says as he un-mutes the TV and gets back to his game.

Johnny hesitates and considers what this means, "So are you going to sit there all day watching baseball?"

Alex looks to Johnny and smiles, "I have my own room, Johnny boy. As soon as you've got the plan for today, I'm outta here."

"So I'm free to do whatever I want?"

"To a point. You can't go all over the world and check things out like Joe did. Remember, he's God, you're not. But you're welcome to walk around and get a feel for Sarah's community and all. Who knows, maybe you'll come across some opportunities to help others out today. That would be cool. Or you can stay in here and watch whatever you want on TV. I can even show you some tricks you might not be aware of in your new world that would really be cool if you want to watch TV." He smiles at Johnny.

"No, no, I'm not much of a TV guy. So if I go out into the community, do you have to follow me?"

Alex laughs, "Oh no, I'm not going to follow you. I can

simply flip channels and keep up with you and only come out if you might need some help."

"But you'll let me know, right? You remember the signal for if others can see you, right?"

Alex laughs again as he shakes his head, "I'm an angel, Johnny boy. I don't forget anything, and I'm here to support you, not to screw up anything you're doing. You're free to do whatever you'd like today and I'll only be there if needed."

Johnny sits on his bed in thought as Alex finishes up, "You'll be fine, Johnny boy. Relax and enjoy the day off."

With that, Alex disappears and the TV goes off, leaving Johnny alone sitting on his bed to consider the day before him.

****

As Johnny is casually strolling around the town square, he seems to be relaxing and getting use to the idea of having the day off. It's a beautiful, crisp day in the mountain community and it's actually a nice change of scenery from what he was use to in his other life. Window shopping and quietly observing the flow of the people is a nice break for Johnny.

Suddenly, Johnny hears an alarm going off from across the town square. He turns and sees some young men jumping into a car in front of the bank and quickly recognizes he is watching a robbery in action. He knows he must act quickly but is hesitant as he's not sure what powers he has in his new world that would be helpful in this situation.

Just as Johnny takes his first step, Alex appears in front of him with his arms raised as if to be stopping Johnny. "Johnny,

Johnny, Johnny! No one can see me or hear me but you, so don't do anything stupid but quietly follow me."

Johnny stops and stares at Alex, who has his hands up and waits to make sure Johnny is paying attention. Johnny, a bit startled, begins to speak, "But there's a bank…."

Alex interrupts quickly, "Nobody sees me Johnny! Do NOT say another word. Just follow me and we'll go somewhere to talk." He holds his finger to his lips to be quiet and make sure Johnny understands.

Johnny watches as the get-away car speeds past them and gets away while people are coming out of the bank screaming for help, then turns back to Alex who remains in a 'be quiet' posture and, once he has Johnny's attention again says, "Follow me,." as he turns to go along the side of the building they were standing in front of.

Johnny watches until Alex turns to him and gestures to 'come on' and Johnny reluctantly takes some steps towards Alex, who turns again and heads to a door on the side of the building and opens it, then waits for Johnny, who quickly enters the doorway then stops and looks around confused. They are back in his hotel room when Alex follows Johnny in and is shaking his head.

"That was a close one, but I think I caught you in time to avoid any embarrassing situations. Listen Johnny boy, you're not Superman. We can't have you being a super hero while you're working for us, okay?"

Johnny reacts a bit offended, "I wasn't trying to be

Superman, I was just going to see if I could help out, that's all."

"Bad idea, Johnny boy. When you're out and about, it's really important for you to remain anonymous and remember what your assignment is. You're here for Sarah's well being, not to play a super hero."

Johnny really doesn't appreciate the reference to being a super hero, "I wasn't going for a super hero, Alex. You said I could take the day off and maybe find other opportunities to help others, and a bank robbery seemed like a pretty good opportunity to do some good, that's all."

"Well that sounds all good, Johnny boy, but what do we do if those guys have guns and in front of the whole township, unloads those guns on you? How do we explain that to Sarah tomorrow when you walk into her room perfectly healthy after all the news has been talking about the good Samaritan who gave up his life to save the day?" he says with that smile.

Johnny pauses and concedes that Alex is making a good point before Alex continues.

"If you want to buy breakfast for some young mothers anonymously, that's great, but you must always do whatever you can to avoid drawing attention to yourself while you're on assignment. You have to remember that as soon as you've accomplished your assignment with Sarah, you will quickly be removed to meet with George to decide your next move. We just can't have the whole township asking about you after you leave. It just makes things more difficult, that's all."

Johnny relaxes as he understands what Alex is talking

about. It makes sense really, and he shudders to think what might have been had Alex not been there to stop him.

"I suppose you're right, Alex, and I do appreciate you being there to save me from a potential disaster. I was just reacting to the situation without thinking it through, I guess."

Alex punches Johnny on the shoulder, "That's okay, Johnny boy. Humans do a lot of stupid things without thinking. That's why I'm here. We angels don't have that super hero desire in us, so we're quite good at jumping into the mix and stopping our human workers before they can screw up an assignment. It's just another reason we make such a good team, Johnny boy."

Johnny sits on his bed, a bit frustrated at how Alex always calls him Johnny boy, how he thinks that he is saving him from some super hero complex, but mostly at how everything Alex says makes sense.

"Well, no harm done, I suppose. I think I understand better how this all works now, so you shouldn't have to worry about it too much moving forward." he says.

"It's all good, Johnny boy. The hardest part for me is following Joe's act. It's always a tough act to follow because…. well…. he's God. He does things that makes most of us angels shudder because we know we'll have to work extra hard to explain his actions are not what you or anyone else working in the program can do. To be honest, none of us angels like to work with clients that have been recruited by God. It's just not fair"

Johnny smiles as he thinks about his friend Joe, "Can you

imagine what he would have done with those bank robbers?" he says with a big smile.

"Exactly, " says Alex, shaking his head, "But that's the point. Joe could have pulled that off without any problems. But you're not Joe, so it's important for you to be reminded that your assignment is Sarah first and foremost. And only your work with Sarah is what the people should know about you."

Alex sees that Johnny understands what has happened, so he wraps it up, "You'll be fine Johnny boy. Just remember to do everything in anonymity or you'll be seeing a lot of me and I'll be missing a lot of baseball. Besides, it's more fun to help people out without them knowing it was you. Embrace that. See how many people you can help out without anyone knowing it was you! That's when you humans really go crazy. I worked with one lady who absolutely went bonkers with helping others out – anonymously. George kept asking her if she was ready for her eternity and her eyes would light up, 'No way – let me have another assignment!' She just loves seeing people get the blessings of enough. She's still out there, too. Remember when you and Joe were walking out of the Pub and you looked back at Sue and saw her expression?" Johnny smiles in reflection, "That's what this program is all about. Of course you can't be like Joe." he pauses as he smiles in thought, "Although, I must say that those people who have the blessing of enough experience from God turn out to be among our best workers on this side. When George informs them that wasn't just Joe the writer doing research helping them out, but actually God, wow! Their hearts melt at the thought and they are always anxious to help with our program here. God may break a lot of the rules and he really does make our work as angels difficult at times, but his heart is always pure and rich. He can frustrate us, but the truth is whatever it is he's doing is being done in the purest form of love, so we learn to just do what we have to do without complaining."

He looks at Johnny and remembers to get back to his point, "But you're not Joe. Or God. Do everything anonymously and let me just watch some baseball games." he says again with that smile.

Johnny is relaxed in understanding, "I think I've got it now, Alex BOY." he says with a pinch of sarcasm.

Alex smiles, "I'm not a boy or a girl, Johnny boy, I'm a spirit," totally missing the sarcasm, "We just put a physical figure in front of you so you don't think you're going mad talking to air. Angel technology, Johnny boy .... angel technology."

With that, Alex disappears as Johnny is left alone, unsure of what he should do. As he is wondering what his next move should be, a voice comes out of nowhere, startling Johnny.

"Oh and Johnny, when you leave your room, you'll be back in the alley where we left off, so if anyone says anything, tell them you heard the alarms and ran down the alley to hide or something. Then go along with your day."

Johnny gathers himself, "You scared the hell out of me! Don't ever do that again."

"That's why I'm Alex, buddy boy. I could just talk to you any time I want, but in order for you to do your job, we like to keep it as humanly real as possible. Have a nice day."

Johnny shakes it off and heads to the door and opens it. Sure enough, he is back in the alley. He pauses, then accepts his surroundings and heads back up to the front. He sees the police cars in front of the bank with people out in front of the various businesses around the town square watching and talking to each other.

"You just missed a bank robbery." says a young lady standing next to Johnny.

Johnny looks at the young lady who is wearing an apron and must be a server at the small bar behind them.

"Actually, I did see it. When the alarms went off and I saw the men getting into the car, so I went down the alley here to avoid being seen."

"Good move," she says, then turns to another lady standing next to her and continues her conversation, "This really sucks because I was going to go to the bank at my break and get some cash out. I have to pick up my car later and the guy won't take anything but cash." she tells her friend.

Johnny pulls out his wallet, thinking he doesn't have anything but his GETA credit card, and sees some cash inside. He cautiously interrupts the young lady, "How much do you need?" he asks her.

She turns to him, "I need to have $120 dollars to get my car, and so far I've only made $40 in tips, I'll have to really work the tips this afternoon."

Johnny counts his cash and realizes he has exactly $80 in cash. He pulls it out and hands it to the girl, "Here, take this and get your car."

She protests, "No sir, I couldn't do that. I'll make it work somehow."

Johnny smiles and says, "I really didn't think I had any cash on me, so this must have just fallen from Heaven." he hears Alex clearing his throat in thin air, "Please take it. It's just enough to insure you get your car without worrying about people tipping you the rest of the day."

"Thank you sir, but I really couldn't. I don't even know you. How could I ever repay you?"

Johnny smiles, " Well my name is Johnny, and the way to repay me is by helping others who come up a few bucks short. Give them enough to smile again."

"This is way more than a few bucks, Johnny." she says.

"Oh, not really." He pauses and reaches his hand out to shake her hand, "What is your name?"

"Sally, " she says as she shakes his hand.

"Yes, Miss Sally, it's all about perspective. I didn't think I had any cash on me and when I looked, I had just enough to help you out. That $80 dollars is going to do a lot more for you today than it would have for me."

Sally's friend jumps in reaching her hand out to Johnny, "My name is Barbara, but everyone calls me Babs. I manage this bar, so how about you come in and I'll buy you a couple drinks, Sally can work the rest of her shift without worrying about the tips and everyone comes out with a smile on their face?"

"Well that sounds good to me." says Johnny as looks to Sally and continues, "So it's up to you, Sally. You can take the money now and just say thank you, or we can go inside and I can have a couple of drinks that Babs won't charge me for and I'll leave her an $80 dollar tip that you could 'borrow' from her." he smiles as Babs looks to Sally smiling in agreement.

Sally looks at them both and hesitates, "I don't know, $80 dollars is a lot of money."

Johnny interrupts, "Well you may think it's a lot of money because of what it can do for you today, but for me, it just got me a couple free drinks at this fine looking bar, and I'm perfectly okay with that."

Babs doesn't wait, "Come on then, let's get back to work. Maybe those bank robbers will come back and spend some of that money here."

The three get a good laugh as they head into the bar. As Johnny settles into his place at the bar – just as his real life, he chooses the end seat near the servers station – Babs pours him a drink and delivers it.

"So Johnny, what brings you to this part of the world? Haven't seen you around. You just passing through?" asks Babs.

"I have a little work to do at the hospital, so I'll be here a couple weeks or so."

"You a doctor?"

"Oh no. I work with head injury patients to get them

emotionally set for the rehab ahead. Head injuries can be frustrating to bounce back from."

At that Babs becomes very interested, "Who are you working with?"

Johnny smiles, "Sorry, I can't tell you. Patient confidentiality, you know."

Babs interrupts, "It's Sarah! You're working with Sarah aren't you?"

Johnny just smiles as Babs doesn't wait for an answer, "Sally and I went to visit her the other day. She said something about a head job guy who was trying to convince her to simply do enough each day instead of trying to constantly push to do more."

Johnny smiles, "Well I find that patients of head injuries do better when they focus on doing enough each day to take another step and not worry about making progress by leaps and bound ."

As Sally heads to the servers station, Babs fills her in.

"Sally, this is the guy Sarah was talking about the other day when we saw her. The head shrink guy."

Johnny begins to protest the head shrink comment, but to no avail.

"Get outta here," says Sally, "Sarah and I have been best friends for like forever. Is she going to be okay, Johnny?"

Johnny pauses in thought. So much for patient confidentiality, but then again, I am suppose to look for opportunities to spread the blessings of enough message to her circle of friends, and these girls may be a big help to me.

"She's a good kid. It's all about having a positive attitude, and I'm thinking Sarah has a good combination of determination and positive attitude to get her through the rehab."

"Well she's not a kid, Johnny, and I do think she has a good attitude and desire to beat this." says Sally as she heads out with another load of drinks for table 4.

Johnny realizes – again – that he nearly blew his cover and how he has to remember that he's not 85 years old on this side. He takes a good pull on his drink at the close call.

"Can I get you another drink, Johnny?" asks Babs.

"No thanks. I think I need to head out for now."

Babs leans over to Johnny, "Sarah is going to be okay, right? Sally and Sarah have been best friends forever and it would really kill Sally if she had any long term affects from this fall."

"I think she's going to be fine. She's young and has a good heart. The important thing for her is to be satisfied with doing enough each day. Most people get into trouble when they get focused on doing more. More exercises. More time. More effort. We live in a world where people always want more. They think that you win by never being satisfied and constantly seeking more. It's like Sally. She can go to bed tonight satisfied that she got enough to get her car back, or she could go to bed frustrated that if she only got a few more tips, she could have had a better day. It's a lesson we all need to remember. Having enough is a good thing. Always wanting more is not. Especially with Sarah situation."

"Those are good words to live by, Johnny," says Babs as she smiles, " But then in my business, I'm use to teaching people that lesson. You've had enough, sir. I am not going to give you more." she laughs, " My livelihood depends on me preaching that lesson of enough, right?"

Johnny smiles, "Yes Babs, that's exactly what I'm talking about. You keep preaching that to Sarah when she gets frustrated and I guarantee you, she will get better."

With that, Johnny gets up to leave as the girls say goodbye. Sally stops what she is doing to come give Johnny a big hug.

"Thanks again for your help, Johnny. I really do appreciate your kindness."

"Just remember when you lay your head on your pillow tonight that it was a good day because you got enough. Appreciate enough, Sally, and you'll always sleep well."

"You just make sure Sarah has enough to get better." Sally says.

"We can all do that, Sally. Make sure Sarah has enough love around her to want to get well. She'll be fine"

With that, Johnny heads out the door and makes his way back to his room. As he sits at his desk reviewing the day and all the twists and turns it gave him, Alex knocks on the door as promised, but walks right in without waiting for a response, with that big smile.

"Johnny boy, ya did well today. Just wanted to let you know that they caught those bank robbers just outside of town without any fuss, so I'm guessing my efforts turned what could have been a disastrous day into a pretty awesome day of helping Sarah, if I may say so myself."

Johnny shakes his head, "I thought angels didn't have egos?" he says.

"Well most angels don't, but I LOVE IT! I think I'll be high-fivin myself all night next door!" he says as he turns to go back to his room.

Johnny smiles as he realizes Alex is starting to grow on him. "Well it's been a good day to be sure. I think I learned a lot today."

Alex turns and smiles, "You learned enough today, Johnny boy – you learned enough."

15

———

The Goodbye

As Johnny heads into the hospital for another visit with Sarah, he reflects on the work that has been done so far and understands that his time is drawing to a close. He and Alex had discussed the assignment last night and Johnny asked Alex how he would know it's time to move on. Alex, in his usual borderline annoying charm, told him that when he opens a door to leave a room and finds himself standing in George's office instead of a hallway, that would be a pretty good indication that the assignment is done.

"Don't worry about it, Johnny boy. It won't be a surprise for you. Your heart will know it's time before you open any doors." He told him with that smile.

Johnny was feeling that things were pretty much coming to a conclusion. Whatever nurse Pooh said to Sarah's parents last week certainly had an impact on them. Their behavior has been very supportive of the medical staff and the treatment plan being implemented for her. The doctors were saying that Sarah's progress has been impressive and they are even talking about her going home possibly this week and start with her outpatient rehab program. And on a personal note, Johnny felt his mission of spreading the message of 'enough' was working well, not only with Sarah, but those family and friends that surround her. He has dropped by Babs bar regularly to get updates from her and Sally, and feels that everyone who surrounds Sarah is moving in the right direction. He honestly felt like there really wasn't much more he could do for her and knew it was time to start wrapping things up with Sarah and prepare her for his inevitable exit.

He knocks on her door and hears a response to come in. Johnny is pleased to find Sarah alone so he can have a nice visit with her. Sarah seems happy to see Johnny as her smile radiates with excitement. She doesn't give Johnny time to take off his coat before starting the conversation.

"I'm glad you're here, Johnny, because I have some good news for you."

"Oh really, did you win the lottery?" he says as he puts away his coat and heads for the chair next to her bed.

"Pretty much . The doctors said I could go home tomorrow." she says bursting with an infectious sense of excitement.

"Really? That is good news." Johnny says with equal excitement.

"Yeah. They were hesitant because I live alone in my apartment, but everything worked out perfect. Sally was saying she needed to find a place to stay for a couple months while her landlord remodeled her duplex, so Dad talked to my apartment manager and rented a two bedroom apartment in the same complex and said he'd pay the rent for a year while I get back on my feet. So Sally and I will be roommates! Dad and Mom are there now with some friends moving my stuff to the new apartment." she says with an excitement that is totally overflowing with joy.

"Wow! That really is great, Sarah. Looks like everything is falling into place." Johnny says as his heart now assures him that George's office is clearly a door or two away, as he continues. "Looks like you won't be needing my services any more, and that's a good thing." he says with a smile.

"I do hope you stay in touch, though, Johnny." says Sarah with a hint of sadness.

"Well Sarah, I don't make any promises to my clients because God only knows where my next assignment might take me. (Alex clears his throat in an annoying interruption) Besides, my job is to position my clients in the best possible attitude to take on the road to recovery and I think we've done some good work these past couple of weeks. Not only with you, but your parents, Sally and others around you. Attitude is everything when it comes to head injuries and understanding that pursuing enough, not more, is everything in the road to recovery. I think I've done enough to get you headed in the right direction."

Sarah smiles at Johnny fondly, "I guess I wanted more, right?"

Johnny smiles, "That's the one addendum to the rule of

enough. You can never have too much love. That's what unconditional love is all about. God will always give you enough love to get you through anything you face, but he'll always have more love if it's needed. Fill your heart with love, Sarah, and you'll never have room for those negative attitudes that bring us down."

"I'm going to miss you Johnny, but I really do appreciate how you taught me to always look for enough. It really does help. There's been many times during my sessions when I have been frustrated because I want to get more done, but then I remember what you say about enough and it helps me to calm down and focus on baby steps. It really does helps a lot. And my journal really helps a lot too, when I'm frustrated. Thank You!"

"You've done well Sarah. Life isn't that complicated. You never know what hand you'll be dealt, but as long as you have a positive heart of love, you can approach any obstacle with a winning attitude. God always gives us enough to win."

Sarah looks at Johnny curiously, "You know, you've been coming here for a couple weeks and I've never asked about your life. I don't know much about you or how you got into this business of working with head injuries. I feel bad. Every time you're here, we're talking about my world and not once have I taken then time to find out what your world is."

Johnny pauses, "Well you know I have a daughter," he says, while his mind scrambles to come up with anything else that would steer the conversation down any other road but his personal life, when a knock on the door comes followed by nurse Pooh, who never waits for a response. As is the norm, nurse Pooh jumps right in and takes over the conversation, which in this case is a much welcomed relief for Johnny.

"Is this man bothering you, Ms Sarah?" she says with a smile at Johnny, "I can have him removed, you know."

Sarah smiles at nurse Pooh, "Aw, nurse Pooh, I'm going to miss you too." she says with a strong dose of admiration.

"Well who told you I was leaving, girl?" Pooh says a bit surprised.

Sarah laughs, "Not you. I'm leaving. The doctor said I could go back home tomorrow!… Wait a minute …. are you leaving too?" she says.

Nurse Pooh hesitates and looks at both of them. "Well I wasn't going to say anything until after you and Johnny left here. I just hate those long, sappy goodbyes ya know. But I guess I let the cat out of the bag, so yes, this is my last week here. I'll be moving on to another assignment."

Sarah looks confused, "Another assignment?"

Nurse Pooh, who would love to talk about anything else, accepts the notion that she has to explain herself, "I work for a nursing company that gives a nurse the opportunity to travel a lot. We take assignments where nurses are needed. The hospital pays your rent, the company pays you very well, and you get to see so many new places around the country. I even spent nine months on a hospital ship off the coast of Africa once with Doctors Without Borders. I love traveling, so it's the perfect job for me. Now let's stop talking about me and see how that blood pressure is doing." she says as she quickly moves back to the here and now.

"Wow, that sounds like a cool job, but don't you ever get tired of traveling around so much?" Sarah asks.

Nurse Pooh doesn't have to think about it, "Girl, do you ever get tired of breathing? If I get tired of traveling – which I don't see any time soon – I can always find a job as a nurse and settle down somewhere. I love the adventure of working as a traveling nurse, so this is one nurse that isn't going to be growing any roots anytime soon."

Sarah looks at both of them, "You both seem to have such interesting jobs. I'm not sure I could do that."

Johnny jumps in, "That's the excitement of life, Sarah. Everybody has their own gift, their own talents. The important thing is for you to learn what your gift is and follow that. As long as you follow your hearts passions, you'll always have enough."

Nurse Pooh looks to Sarah, "Have you had any conversation with this man where he didn't mention ENOUGH?" They all laugh as nurse Pooh follows up, "He's right though Sarah. God will always give you enough to get you by."

Pooh turns to Johnny, "So now that Sarah has had enough of you, are you leaving as well?"

Johnny laughs, "Yes. For every client that has had enough of me, there's always a client out there who wants more."

Nurse Pooh starts to head for the door, her job done, then turns back to Sarah, "Girl, you take good care of yourself. I think God has a special gift for you. Nice getting to know both of you."

With that nurse Pooh exits the room. Johnny looks to Sarah, who has watery eyes and is looking at the door, before she draws her attention to Johnny and smiles, "I guess that was a long, sappy goodbye for her." as they both laugh.

"Well in her line of work, it probably is a good idea for her not to get too attached to her patients. I'm sure she's had a lot of goodbyes." Johnny says.

"So are you going to just leave as well?" Sarah asks Johnny.

Johnny smiles, "Not without a hug." he says as he gets up to give Sarah a nice hug. As they hug, another knock on the door. It's Sally who comes in bursting with energy.

"Oh, hey Johnny. Hope I'm not interrupting anything." she says as Johnny breaks from the hug and heads to retrieve his coat.

"Not at all. I was just saying goodbye to Sarah."

Sally stops and looks at Johnny, "Are you leaving?"

"Yes Sally, I think Sarah has had enough of me. Time to move on."

With that Sally comes and gives Johnny a big hug, "We're going to miss you Johnny."

"You just make sure she gets enough hugs and she'll be fine." He smiles at Sally and winks, "And a kick in the butt when she starts whining. You both will be fine. It's been a treat getting to know you." He says as he heads for the door.

"Thanks, again, Johnny for all your help," Sarah says, "I've really learned a lot from you."

Johnny turns to Sarah and smiles, "You've learned enough, Sarah."

With that he opens the door and steps into George's office again.

"Well it appears that my assignment is done" he thinks as he looks around and sees George sitting at a desk with a broad smile.

16

———

The Review

"Johnny, come sit down. You did a great job with Sarah, especially for your first assignment. Take a load off your feet and let's review." says George as Johnny makes his way to his seat.

"So I trust you feel pretty good about your first assignment?" asks George.

"It went well. I think Sarah's going in the right direction and she has a good support system around her to keep her on track."

"Yes, it looks as if Sarah is on the right track, indeed. And how about you? How do you feel about your involvement?"

"I think I did okay. I was just being myself, really. I think a lot of credit goes to nurse Pooh. I'm not sure what she said to Sarah's parents, but boy did they turn around. That was important." Johnny says in reflection.

"Yes, I love using Prescott. That woman gets things done for sure."

"Excuse me?" says Johnny, a bit confused.

"Well Johnny, I always like to use other recruits when a new recruit has their first assignment. If I can snag Nurse Prescott, I know it's going to be a great outcome." George says with a big smile.

"Nurse Pooh is a recruit like me?"

"No offense Johnny, but nurse Pooh is a recruit like no other I have. She's a real spitfire and I know if she's on an assignment, things are going to be fine."

Johnny is still a bit unsure, "So Alex is an angel who likes baseball and likes to annoy me, and nurse Pooh is actually a recruit like me who just happened to be on the same assignment as me? Is there anyone else I should know about?"

George sits back in his chair. "Oh no Johnny. You have to look at the big picture here. People on this planet were created with a wonderful gift of free will. Every individual is encouraged to find their own passions and develop their passions to the benefit of many. God is love, and the problem is that the free will has developed this perception of God and religion that creates a great competition between good and evil. God against the devil. One religion teaching against another religion teachings. Johnny, it's not a competition. God doesn't win or lose, God pursues every heart and will never stop pursuing until every heart is a heart of love. My job is to do whatever I can to make every assignment have the greatest potential to win another heart to love. With free will we may not always be successful, but I assure you, we never lose a heart. It may not be this assignment, it may not be this lifetime, but I assure you Johnny, we never lose a heart. That's what unconditional love is all about."

George pauses to let Johnny take this all in before he continues. "Alex is an angel I use all the time with new recruits. He may be a bit annoying at times, but he is very affective in showing new recruits the ropes. He's absolutely fascinated by Earth people and all their gadgets and games. I call him my Earth Angel. He really loves helping out new recruits on Earth."

"Nurse Prescott, now she's a great recruit. God keeps checking with me to see if she wants to move on to her own eternity, but she always turns me down. She absolutely loves working her assignments and I tell God that I'm pretty sure she's already in heaven, so we'll just keep giving her assignments. She was a nurse in her real life and she has no plans to every change. If an assignment involves any medical issues, I always try to get Prescott involved if I can. She really is a great recruit for me."

"Well she certainly deserves most of the credit for this assignment, that's for sure. I'm not sure how much success I would have had with Sarah's parents. Not like she did anyway." says Johnny.

"Oh Johnny, we all get the credit. Again, there's no competition here. We are all pursuing hearts of love. We all have gifts to bring to every assignment. You did great, Alex did great and so did Prescott. God's love is stronger now and that's a good thing. That's the only thing that matters."

Johnny sits back and considers all that has been said. It

all makes sense as he thinks about it. Everything George has talked about is really consistent with what he was thinking as he was growing older in his life on Earth. The whole idea of heaven and hell, good against evil, God versus Satan. It just seemed to be missing the point of what God and unconditional love should be about.

Johnny is feeling more relaxed with a keen sense of appreciation for the understanding he has gained through his first assignment. He knows he has to decide whether to take another assignment or move on. "So where do we go from here?" he asks George.

"It's your call. I have plenty of assignments that you are welcome to pursue, or you are more than welcome to move on to your eternity if you wish." George responds without any tone of pressure one way or another.

"If I take another assignment, will I have another angel? Will there be other recruits working with me?" Johnny asks.

"Every assignment is unique, Johnny. Your first assignment was designed to give you a good feeling for how the program works. My job is to do whatever I can to give each assignment a chance to succeed. If it takes more than one recruit, I'll get them, or it may be an assignment that you can handle on your own. I will always let you know before you take an assignment if there will be others involved so you can maximize your opportunities to succeed. If you're doing an assignment on your own, there will always be an angel available to help you decide if you might need another recruit to help out if need be. There is always an angel to oversee every assignment that will be there at the very beginning to help you plan out the direction your assignment needs to go and what you are most comfortable with in using your angel during the assignment."

Johnny interrupts, "How to use my angels?"

"Yes. With your first assignment you had Alex because every new recruit needs him to show them what they can or can't do. Alex works with every new recruit. From this point on, however, the angels you'll be working with are assigned to the individual on Earth who needs our help. It's the angels that makes the request to me for a recruit because they understand what their person is going through and knows that they are at a critical cross road in their life that may need our recruits to help out. So you'll start each assignment by meeting with the angel assigned to the individual who can explain to you what is going on and come up with a plan that gives you the best chance to succeed. Every angel will observe the progress of the assignment without interfering, but will be connected to your heart so that if there is a need for them to be in your hotel room to go over anything, they can be there. Obviously, an angel assigned to Nurse Prescott only needs to meet her at the beginning and fill her in on what's going on and then leave her alone and let her do her thing. Of course, that is the norm for most recruits who have several assignments under their belt. It usually takes three or four assignments before a recruit truly understands the program and the possibilities they have to make a difference in people's journey on Earth.

Most recruits only need the initial contact with the assigned angel to review the circumstances and come up with a plan, then leave them alone to do their assignment. If you stay with us for a bit, I'm sure that will be true for you as well."

Johnny again considers everything being said and again takes comfort in how it all make sense.

"So if I want to take another assignment, you'll have a couple for me to choose from, then I get together with the individual's angel to develop a game plan, right?" he asks.

"Pretty much. I have many assignments available, but I know your heart so I narrow it down to a couple assignments I feel would be right down your alley. When you choose the one you want, you will walk through that door (he points to a side door) and be greeted by your angel to develop your plan."

Johnny is feeling it and thinks it would be good to try another assignment now that he understands the program.

"Let's see what you got. I'm ready to give it a go again." he says to George.

George smiles as he knows it's always good for recruits to do a couple assignments before they really understand what the program is all about.

They go over the four assignments George feels would be a good fit for Johnny, who is intrigued by all of them and can see why George chose them. But there is one in particular that Johnny wants to pursue.

"I think I'd like to go with this one here. This guy sounds

like a really good guy with a lot on his plate." Johnny says as he hands the assignment sheet to George.

George looks at it and smiles, "Yes, I thought you'd like this one. He's a single parent who lost his wife to cancer. He has absolutely no skills in cooking, housekeeping, laundry. He was raised in the old school of working hard and let the wife do everything else. He's got a long ways to go, but he mostly needs to learn how to be a good Dad. You're message of seeking enough will be great."

He hands the sheet back to Johnny and tells him to go through the door to plan his assignment.

As he's heading for the door, George reminds him, "Johnny – teach him to cook enough and to love his girls more."

Johnny waves his hands without looking back, "Sounds like the right plan, George" as he opens the door and begins his next assignment.

17

———

The Second Assignment

As Johnny walks through the door, he is greeted by not one angel, but two. He looks at both with a bit of confusion on his face as the one angel moves quickly to ease his confusion.

"Welcome, Johnny. My name is Mary and I'm Pete's personal angel. This is Katherine. She was Sue's personal angel. Sue was Pete's wife who passed away, so she will be a lot of help to us as we develop a good plan for Pete."

Now that he understands, Johnny relaxes and greets the two angels. They take their seats at a simple table that has a stack of photographs, which strikes Johnny as a bit odd.

"First we'll go over these pictures so you can see who you are working with," says Mary as she takes the pictures.

"You can't just point and have a slide show appear in the air?" Johnny asks with a touch of humor and a dose of curiosity.

Mary looks to Katherine, " Another Star Wars fan," she says shaking her head, then turns to Johnny, "Well Alex probably would, but I prefer to make my plans without all the 'bells and whistles', I think you call them? Keep the focus on Pete and the plan without any distractions, you know."

Johnny smiles, "Of course."

Mary goes over each picture and gives a simple background info for all the players, with Katherine filling in as well.

What Johnny is coming to understand is that Pete is a good man, but with a very limited skill set for being a single dad. His frustration is fueled by too much competitive testosterone growing up that encouraged him to be a mans man and girls simply belonged in the kitchen and taking care of the kids.

Sue was the perfect wife for Pete. She loved to cook and take care of things around the house even though she worked every bit as hard at her job as an accountant for the local car dealership. But mostly, Sue loved her family. She loved Pete with all her heart and her two girls were the joy of her life.

Johnny listens to the angels speak about the family and what a devastating loss it was when Sue passed away after a difficult struggle with cancer. He understands that this is not going to be an easy assignment, but he also knows that there is a clear path that could be taken to get Pete in the right position to succeed.

"What kind of support system does Pete have? Family, friends, church? Our approach should be to utilize the good support he has as well as caution for the support that doesn't help him." Johnny says.

"Well, the good news is that Pete and Sue were very much

loved in their community." Mary says, "Pete owned his own repair shop locally and had a strong reputation of being a good mechanic who treated his customers right. When Sue got cancer, the owner of the dealership she worked at really stepped up. He is a very popular figure in the community who made a name for himself as a baseball player. After baseball, he settled down in the community and had enough money to own several businesses. He has a reputation of taking care of his employees and people around town know that if you work at one of Mr. Jones businesses, you had a great job. When Sue got the cancer, it was Mr. Jones who talked Pete into working at the dealership as a manager of the repairs department so he could have a stable income and medical benefits for himself and the girls. Pete kept his repair shop and let his long time buddy, Mike – who worked there- take over and run the shop while he took over the day to day activities at the dealership. So financially, Pete is going to be okay. He works for a man – Mr. Jones – who is very supportive and gives Pete all the flexibility he needs to manage the girls at home and the teachers at the girls school have been really supportive as well. So there is a solid foundation within his community that should be of great benefit to Pete."

Mary pauses to see if Johnny has any thoughts, before she continues.

"As to family, Pete doesn't have much there. His dad owns a farm a few hundred miles away and his brother helps him work the farm. Good people, but not very social. They aren't likely to have much impact with Pete's new environment."

Mary looks to Katherine, who takes up the conversation on cue. "Sue's family is big city people. Dad's a lawyer, Mom's a socialite in the big city. They have another daughter who owns a travel agency and is traveling all over the world most the time. Sue and her sister, Stephanie, were close even though they both took very different paths – Stephanie the younger, more adventurous type wanted to travel the world, while Sue was the more quiet one who just wanted to settle down and have a family. They really loved each other and though she was traveling a lot, Stephanie always made time to visit her sister and nieces whenever she could. She got along well with Pete and should be more supportive for Pete after her sisters passing. Mom & Dad were good parents. I see them as on the fence, really. If Pete has a lot of difficulty with the girls, I could see them making his life miserable. They both have the money and the position to interfere and they love their granddaughters. They are not going to sit idle and let the care of the girls go south. They were not overjoyed with Sue marrying a mechanic, but through the years have softened to at least admitting that Pete is a good man who loves his family. That's why we asked George to send help. We really believe if we can keep Pete on a positive path, there is a good chance that Sue's parents could become a very strong support for Pete. This is a critical time, to be sure."

The angels sit back to give Johnny a moment to take in all they have shared.

"Well it sounds like they are in a difficult situation, but I also feel as if there is enough positive support around Pete to keep him going. What do you see as the biggest issue holding Pete back?" asks Johnny.

"His attitude," says Katherine without hesitation, "He was raised to be a strong man and losing his wife, whom he loved very much, was enough of a blow to his spirit. But when you consider the fact he can't cook a lick, sucks at laundry and basic chores around the house and he's on his own with two girls in elementary school, this is one stressed out young man who sees no way out of the tunnel." Katherine says shaking her head.

Mary is quick to follow up, "Fear of failing is where that defeatist attitude comes from. True, he was raised to be tough and strong no matter what, but he also has a very soft side to him that really loved his wife and is just crazy about his girls. It's that love he has that is truly broken and creates this deep fear in his heart that he is going to lose everything. It's not going to be easy to help Pete see the hope when there is so much fear inside. He gets short with the girls over little things and almost always goes to bed feeling overwhelmed with frustration."

Johnny pauses in thought before he speaks, "So what do you see as my role in this?"

Mary is quick to reply, "Katherine and I discussed this and feel that it would be best if you were a new hire in the repair shop. An older mechanic nearing retirement who loves to work on cars and has plenty of miles on his resume to become a good source of advice to his boss, Pete. We feel it's important for Pete to have someone around who has experience and is able to simplify all the issues that overwhelm Pete and get him thinking positively about his abilities to overcome the issues."

Johnny smiles as he sits back, "Well I know you angels are busy, but I feel you need to understand I know absolutely nothing about cars. That's why I started taking the bus after Beth passed away."

Katherine is quick to jump on that statement, "Oh Johnny, please. You have to understand you are on this side now. We didn't ask George to send us a good mechanic, we wanted someone who could be a mechanic of Pete's heart. Whatever role we decide on, you'll be an expert at because our focus will always be on Pete and getting his heart right. You didn't know much about head injuries when you helped Sarah, right? Stop thinking in terms of your life on Earth and understand that you are on this side now and we want you to help us help Pete. Of course you won't be much help if you're an idiot who knows nothing about cars. We'll cover you on all that stuff. You just have to stay focused on Pete and his girls."

Johnny sits back a little humbled at Katherines comments. It takes some getting use to working with angels like Alex and Katherine because they sure don't hold back on anything, that's for sure. But then again, that's what angels should do, so he figures it is best to listen and keep in mind that everything that is said is for Pete and what we can do to help him out.

"You're right, Katherine. I suppose I do have a knack for my thoughts slipping to my past. I apologize."

Katherine smiles at Johnny, "It's okay, you're not the first one to do this. You just have to remember that you are working for God now and trust that God is never going to let you do anything foolish. If we decide that you are a mechanic, then I guarantee you will be the best mechanic at the dealership regardless of your past life. We always play to win hearts, Johnny"

Johnny understands the mission better now as the three get focused on the plan for Johnny.

18

——

The Pit

As Johnny gets out of his car for the first day of 'work' at the dealership, he's feeling pretty good about the set up. He is glad the angels let him keep the basic profile from his days on the other side. His name will be Johnny, his wife, Beth, died ahead of him and his daughter Elizabeth is a traveling doctor. He can approach this assignment at least knowing he won't have to scramble to correct something he says out of context.

As he goes inside the car drop off bay, he sees Pete at the counter with a cup of coffee going over accounts for the day. Pete notices Johnny and comes out from behind the counter to greet him.

"Johnny, good to see you. Welcome to the pit, as we like to call it" he says as he extends his hand to shake. "We'll start out in the office here to go over all that necessary business stuff before I show you around and get you going."

Pete leads Johnny into a small office that doesn't appear to be used much. Simple layout with very little clutter. As they both sit down, Pete offers Johnny a cup of coffee, which he declines, before he cuts to the quick.

"I know you have a ton of experience and you'd probably prefer to just get to work, so I'll try not to take up too much of your time getting all this business stuff out of the way."

Johnny smiles, "No problem. It is was it is."

"It's a pain, that's what it is. Some times I wish I could just spend every day under the hood of a car, but it is necessary to get all this taken care of, so I'll try not to take too long with it."

Pete goes over all the forms and legal business that needs to be done with a new hire. Johnny is paying attention, not to all the legal nonsense, but looking for opportunities to insert a message to Pete that he would be a good source to talk to. But it becomes obvious that Pete really didn't like this part of his job as he was very business like and seemed anxious to just get it over with.

No worries for Johnny. He knows this was just the beginning and there would likely be many windows of opportunities to gently let Pete know that he is available. After all, he's working on the other side now and is certain that the timing is ripe now because Pete's heart is ready to receive the message he needs to get on a positive path. Johnny can be patient and learn more by simply observing.

With the paperwork finished, Pete seems relieved to have that behind him as they get up for a tour of the facility. Again, Pete is very business like and never ventures into any casual conversations.

Johnny is realizing that Pete is very much the kind of leader who keeps his focus on the business and makes no attempt to show a 'buddy' quality as many bosses like to do. He can see that Pete has a good heart as he presents the rules of the pit without any sense of fear, but more of a softer tone as he explains why these rules are important for the good of the whole shop. He is thorough in explaining the responsibilities of each person, and does so with a demeanor that is calm and non-threatening.

"Let's go check out your work space and I can introduce you to your co-workers." Pete says as he gets out of his chair.

They get out to the pit, as they call it, and Pete stops to give Johnny a general overview.

"We have eight stations here – four on each side. You'll have the first one here. Next to you is Suzy – I call her my Pit Bull because that girl loves to get in there and fix cars. If I get a difficult job, I always try to get it to Suzy. Next to her is Jacks station. He's a great trouble shooter who is also one funny guy. I put him next to Suzy on purpose because they are my extroverts and with them feeding off each other all day long, this shop never gets boring. And at the end is Joe. He started out in the body shop and was their best worker, but he kept telling them he wanted to do more than pop dents. He wanted to work on engines too. They finally gave in and he's made quite a reputation for us here. Whenever he's done with a job, he always goes around and pops any dents before he releases the car. We have a great reputation for going that extra mile, but in truth, it's just Joe being Joe.

If he sees a car with a dent that he can fix, he's on it. On this side, across from you is Anna . She can fix anything electrical. All my mechanics are great working on engines, but they all have their own areas of expertise. If there is an electrical or computer issue, Anna is the one you want. She actually does a lot of side jobs installing sound systems in cars and could probably make decent career just doing that, but she likes working on engines too, not to mention the benefits we give her, so she's happy. Next to her is Harvey. He's been working on cars forever and just loves it. A quiet guy but a good guy who really knows his stuff. Then we have JC. No one knows what his real name is – well I do, but if he wants keep it secret, I'll go with it. He's a great mechanic and if you ask him what JC stands for, he'll smile and say Jesus Christ and move on. I don't think he cares about his real name, I think he just gets a kick out of saying it's Jesus Christ. He's kind of a quiet guy, but he has a really dry sense of humor. He and Jack are best of friends. Then at the end is Lou. He's a quiet, shy guy who really enjoys his work and is the one I go to with anything related to brakes, wheel alignment, anything under the car and Lou's my go-to guy."

Pete takes a breather to see if Johnny has any questions before he continues.

"I have a shop of really good mechanics and I insist that they leave their egos at the door. The most important statistic for me is a zero return policy. I do not want cars returned to me because it wasn't fixed properly. If you're having trouble, get another mechanics input or help. I want two signatures on the work sheet – one from the mechanic who did the work, and one from a mechanic who checked it out. I tell them that we are all responsible for every car that comes in here and as long as I'm here, there will never be individual awards or bonuses. We are one unit and we will all be rewarded for our work as a team. Let's go meet your coworkers."

As Pete introduces him to the other mechanics in the shop, Johnny takes a quick read of each individual and it becomes clear that Pete has assembled a quality crew for the dealership. Five men and two women who carry themselves well and are friendly. Johnny can tell right away that this is a group of people that you would want to work with.

Pete shows Johnny to his work space and explains what he should expect to do each day when he comes to work.

"Well that's about it for now, Johnny. I don't have anything for you to work on today unless something comes up, so you can read through all the legal stuff I gave you or just walk around and get to know your co-workers. Harvey has been here the longest, JC is just a couple months here. The others are somewhere in-between."

With that, Pete leaves Johnny to head back to his work as Johnny begins his adventures of a master mechanic who knows nothing about cars.

19

___

The Frustration

As Johnny settles into his new routine at the dealership, he is learning to enjoy the comradery of his new co-workers. Pete's take on everyone in the shop was spot on. After only his first week, Johnny can see that Pete is a very perceptive boss to work for. He knows when to back off and let the crew work and when to jump in and gently get their attention focused on the work. When the debate gets testy, Pete is good about coming around and reminding them that they are not here to solve the problems of the world, but are here to solve the problems of our cars. He is definitely a boss you want to work for.

He never corrects someone, he teaches. There have been a couple of instances already when he has had everyone stop what they were doing to come look at a job someone else was having trouble with. He wants everyone to learn from the problems that come up and is good about building a team atmosphere in the pit.

Johnny is enjoying the work at the dealership. Every day when he gets a new job, he is amazed at how much he is able to understand the problem and is able to make the proper diagnosis to getting the car back to 100%. He is constantly smiling as he remembers when he was on the other side, his idea of fixing a car was to check the air in the tires and if that didn't work, take it to a mechanic. It's a whole new world opened up for Johnny and he is really enjoying it.

He is getting more comfortable with his co-workers too. Pete was right about Suzy and Jack being together. They really are the spark plugs of the pit that draws out the rest of the workers. He is certain that the others would be happy to quietly go about their business, but Suzy and Jack have a great way of pulling everyone into the conversation. Pete doesn't want any distractions and Johnny finds it interesting how there is no music. You are allowed to wear earphones, but Johnny hasn't seen any since he started. Everybody is involved in the moment and with Suzy and Jack keeping things light and lively, who needs music.

Johnny can even tell the effect they have on him. He finds himself more relaxed in the pit and willing to participate with the others in a more open manner than when he was on the other side. Getting use to his new found knowledge of mechanics certainly helps him to relax, but he is beginning to realize that not only is there no job that he can't fix, but also how the mix of personalities in the shop has brought out more personality in his own self than he ever thought he had.

Johnny thinks of the days when he'd hang at the Pub

and how he seldom contributed to a conversation unless someone pulled it out of him. He was always more content to quietly observe life and was never anxious to participate in any conversations. He knows work as an engineer for all those years was ideal for him because his work days were spent quietly problem solving and creating.

It has made Johnny think about working on the other side of life. Could it be that not only is he given this new knowledge about working on cars, but maybe he is given a different personality that fits more into the environment that he is working? Or could it be that he always had that personality but never had the environment that allowed it to grow?

When he worked with Sarah on his last assignment, Johnny felt pretty much like the Johnny he was in real life, just a younger version. He doesn't remember his personality being much different than it was in real life. Johnny is certain that if Alex was his angel in this assignment, he would pop into Johnny's head and tell him that he's over thinking this and to stay focused on helping Pete.

Come to think of it, Johnny hasn't heard or seen Mary or Katherine since he started this assignment. He guesses that could be good news as he is sure he'd hear from them if he was doing something wrong. Angels don't seem to be the kind that would let an assignment go south without jumping in.

Which gets Johnny thinking about the assignment. He's suppose to be working with Pete, but the truth is that Pete hasn't given Johnny much opportunity to get personal with him. When he's at work, he remains very business like. He works on a very even level of emotion. It's nearly impossible to tell if he is in a good mood or a bad mood. Very friendly guy who always stays in the moment and so far, Johnny has never heard him talk about his personal life.

After working here for a week, Johnny gets the impression that this is true with all the co-workers as well. Everyone seems to stay in the moment. Johnny hasn't heard very much conversation from anyone about their personal life. No one has asked Johnny about his life either. It is truly a shop that just talks about cars.

As Johnny gets into his car, he is a bit hesitant. It's been another great day working on cars and participating with co-workers in the daily issues, but once again he leaves work without any opportunities to plant any seeds of hope for Pete. Johnny is feeling bad for Pete as he thinks of how Pete goes home every night to his girls and struggles to feed them and get their nightly routines going by himself while he has done nothing to help him. Somehow Johnny can't help but think that this wasn't part of the plan.

As he pulls out of the dealership, Johnny notices Mary hitchhiking on the side of the road. Johnny quickly pulls over as Mary jumps in.

"What are you doing hitchhiking, for crying out loud? People don't hitchhike any more!" Johnny says to Mary in a baffled tone.

Mary turns and smiles, "No one can see me but you, so you

might want to move on before people freak out at the guy on the side of the road talking to himself."

Johnny panics as he hurriedly pulls away, nearly cutting off a car that zooms by. Once Johnny settles into a more relaxed state of driving, he turn back to Mary to continue.

"What are you doing here?"

"Well you seemed to be a bit confused about your assignment and I thought I'd pop in and let you know everything is going great." She says with very little emotion.

"Great? How can you say things are going great when I haven't done one thing to help Pete out? That guy doesn't give you a window of opportunity any time at work. When he's at the shop, he's all business." Johnny says with a good dose of frustration.

Mary responds casually, "Well that is his job, you know. He's in charge of eight mechanics and making sure those cars get fixed properly. It's not like he has all day to sit back and shoot the breeze, I think they call it."

Johnny looks over to Mary a bit confused, then back at the road ahead, "So what part of all this makes you say that everything is going great?"

"Oh Johnny, you worry too much. You have to remember this is a free will planet. People can choose to go the right way, or the wrong way, it's up to them. We angels don't have crystal balls, ya know. We can't see into the future. We brought you into this assignment because Pete was at a critical time in his life, and we needed you to be available if things started going the wrong way. But so far, Pete seems to be adjusting pretty well to his new world and his support system seems to be doing better than expected. So far, so good."

"Well it just seems like I'm wasting my time here. How will I know it's time to go if I'm not doing anything?"

Mary laughs, "Oh Johnny, you humans are such a delight. There is no time on this side, so you're not wasting anything. Your fixing cars – and doing a pretty good job for a guy who doesn't know anything about cars, " she pauses and smiles at Johnny who looks at her with a face of contempt, "I'm Pete's angel and I'm feeling good about how things are going. George will know when it's time for you to go back. Until then, enjoy the work and plant those seeds of hope to Pete or anyone else while you're here. You're not being graded on this assignment. It has no affect on your eternity, so relax, Johnny and enjoy the ride. If you get the opportunity, great. If not, great. This assignment is about Pete, not you. And so far Pete is doing well – that's all that matters."

With that, Mary smiles at Johnny, then disappears. Johnny nearly runs off the road but recovers quickly. He's not sure how many assignments he'll take on , but he will never get use to the angels coming and going as they do. He has a feeling they do that on purpose to mess with humans.

As Johnny drives on, he thinks about what Mary said and must admit it makes sense. He begins to understand that he is thinking too much in a selfish manner and if Pete is doing well, he should just be happy for him.

As Johnny rolls into his hotel to settle in for the evening, he does a lot of thinking about the day. It seems with every day there is something new to learn about working on the other side of life. The angels may not be the most tactful creatures, but they do make sense every time he talks with them. It's easy to get wrapped up in your own feelings and all, but the truth is that he is only here to help Pete out.

Starting tomorrow, Johnny is going to relax more and simply enjoy the assignment. If Pete, or anyone else, gives him an opportunity to share the message of enough, he'll take it. If not, he'll simply enjoy working on cars and the fellowship of the seven friends he works with.

As Johnny sits back with a nightcap, he smiles and thinks about starting a new tradition for himself. Just to keep his sense of humor, before he signs off on any job, he's going to check the air in the tires first!

20

______

The Passing

Johnny pulls into the dealership for another day and is feeling better about his assignment. Since his visit with Mary, Johnny has learned to relax more and understand that an assignment on this side of life doesn't need you to be anxious about getting results. It is a free will world, after all, and all you can do is simply look for windows of opportunity to plant the seeds of enough whenever you can. He keeps reminding himself of what Mary said to him- that he is not being graded on this assignment and that whatever happens will have no impact on his own eternity. It's so easy to get into the mind set that this is his assignment and he needs to get results. But it really is Pete's assignment and Johnny is merely a part of his support team to help him in his new world as a single parent.

Johnny is enjoying his work more now. It really is a treat for him to work on these cars and he's learning to appreciate the whole world of auto mechanics. Johnny knew nothing about how cars worked when he was on the other side, but having this assignment has taught him so much, not just in how to fix cars and make them run better, but in the possibilities these assignments have to give you experiences that you never imagined on the other side.

As Johnny gets settled into his station and with his co-workers normal conversations, Pete comes on the intercom and tells all of them to come to his office for a brief meeting before we get started. This is not unusual for Pete, as he is prone to call a quick meeting to go over something so he doesn't have to repeat it over again to all of us individually.

As they gather in his office, Pete, as is the case every time he calls a meeting, doesn't like to waste time, starts, when Suzy interrupts.

"Don't you want to wait for Jack? He hasn't come in yet." she says.

Pete pauses and looks at Suzy and gets right to the point. "Jack won't be coming in today. He passed away last night."

Suzy blurts out a loud " WHAT?" as the rest of the mechanics freeze in disbelief.

"I spoke with his wife, Jane, last night. It was a sudden heart attack and there was nothing anyone could do."

Pete stops to let this all sink in. Suzy sits in one of the two chairs in the office as JC comes over to sit next to her and holds her. The rest of them are just numb of emotion.

"I know this is a big blow to us here at the pit and unfortunately, we do have cars sitting out there and customers who expect us to get their cars back to them in a timely matter. You are the best team of mechanics I could ever hope to have and I trust each one of you 100%. Until I say differently, I don't want any of you to clock out for lunches – Go to lunch when you need the break and come back when you're ready to work on cars again. I'll make sure that each of your time cards reflect the normal time for lunch. If you need a break, take it, if you need to talk, talk to someone, if you need to cry, cry. I know from experience that everyone deals with grief differently, so I promise each of you that I will give you the space and time you need to get through this. I know how much each one of you loves to work on cars, so I'm not worried about anyone taking advantage of the situation. But I ask each one of you to communicate to one another. Help each other out. Let's be there for each other during this time, but let's continue to deliver these cars back to our customers in perfect shape."

Pete pauses to see if anyone has anything to say. Everyone continues to just be numb, so Pete concludes by looking at those who are standing.

"If it's okay with you, I'm going to have Suzy and JC stay in here with me for awhile, if you guys want to go ahead and get to your stations. I'll come out in a bit to work at Jack's station."

With that, the mechanics quietly head out to the pit. They instinctively stop in the middle as Anna is the first to break the silence.

"Man, nobody saw that coming. This is going to be tough for us." she says.

Surprisingly, Lou is the one who takes charge. "Maybe we

should all see where each car is in their repairs and work together to get these cars out of here. I'm about done with the one I'm working on, so I can get mine out in a half hour, then I can help anyone else out to get their car out too. Maybe if we team up and work together, we won't be too distracted."

Anna is quick to respond, "That's a good idea Lou. What if I help you finish up your car, so you can help me get my car done. I really feel like I'm going to need to be working with others at least today or I'll be a basket case."

Harvey jumps in, "I'll check JC's job out – I think he was almost done with his." he looks to Johnny, "Johnny, maybe you could check out Suzy's job and see where she stands."

"I'm in pretty good shape, so I'll check out Jack's job and see where he was at." says Joe.

Just hearing Jack's name gives everyone a somber pause.

"God I'm going to miss that man. We've got to make sure his wife and daughter are taken care of." says Anna as she walks with Lou down to his station, and the rest of them head to theirs.

Johnny starts thinking that this possibly could have been pre-arraigned in order to give him more opportunities while he's on assignment, so he better keep his eyes and ears open, when suddenly Mary's voice comes blasting into his head.

"Oh come on Johnny! You think God killed Jack so you could have something to talk about while you wait for Pete to open up? Oh Pah-leeeeeeeeese Johnny! Get over yourself or I'll ship you back to George in a heartbeat! STOP IT!"

Well she didn't have to get so testy, but of course she

is right. We humans certainly have a crazy way of tying these disasters with God trying to teach us something. Johnny definitely has to shake off any thoughts of that being the case here.

They all spend a little time checking out all the cars to see which ones they can get out today. It really is good that they are working together and keeping their minds on the work in front of them. It's pretty clear that everyone here will go home tonight and have an emotional melt down, but for now the best medicine seems to be work.

As they settle into their work, Pete, JC and Suzy come into the pit to take their place. Anna explains the plan that they came up with to get through the day and the three agree that it's the best plan considering the circumstances.

The morning quickly becomes busy with everyone helping each other with the cars. There is more conversation as each of them keeps the others updated on the progress of the cars being worked on. Even Pete seems to be enjoying rolling up his sleeves and getting his hands dirty as he goes from station to station to help others, though he does get called away often by calls and other managerial responsibilities that need his attention.

When Pete returns from another business interruption, he tells everyone not to make lunch plans as they will all be taken care of.

About an hour later, Mr. Jones walks into the pit. This is the first time Johnny has ever seen the owner since he started, but understands this is normal for him. Being that he owns other businesses in the community and his celebrity status as a former major league baseball player, he's not likely to have much time to spare.

Pete gets everyone to stop what they are doing, as he knows why Mr. Jones is here.

"I know you all are busy, but I picked up some lunch for you all and threw everyone out of the break room, so we have it all to ourselves. Let's take a break and eat while it's still hot." he says.

Mr. Jones waits at the door leading towards the break room as they all scramble to clean up. It's clear from the conversations being bantered about that this is not a typical occurrence. Suzy tosses out that she didn't even know they had a break room, which seemed like a typical response from these grease monkeys – as they like to call themselves. Johnny suspects as good a team as they are, they probably have no idea who the people are working at the dealership outside of the pit.

As they all make their way to the break room, they are greeted by a spread of food that is quite impressive. Mr. Jones, not surprisingly, is having our lunch catered. Bar-B-Que, Fried Chicken and all the works with a couple of servers to keep our plates full. He even knows what each mechanic likes to drink as there is a good variety of soft drinks and beer.

They all settle in and fill their plates. Mr. Jones sits down with a plate already made and announces, "One of the perks of owning the business is that I got to make my plate before I came and got you. I always get the best parts of the chicken." he says with that engaging smile he's known for.

As they all dig in, there seems to be no rush. Mr. Jones is enjoying his food and goes around to each of the mechanics to ask where they're from and get to know them. He seems more interested in listening than he is talking. It is no surprise to see why everyone wants to work with this guy as he is so personable and easy to talk to.

As Mr. Jones finishes his lunch, he stands up to talk. "I know you all have suffered a great loss today and I wanted you to know that my pain is in not knowing Jack like you all did. From what Pete tells me, Jack was the spark plug that kept the pit running. I truly am sorry about your loss and I don't pretend to be smart enough to have any magical words to make you feel any better."

"I want you to know that this dealership is committed to taking care of Jack's wife and daughter. I have spoken with Jane and assured her that we will take care of all the arraignments and that I will personally make sure her daughter has whatever education she wants."

"I have spoken with Pete and am fully supportive of his handling of the situation. I am well aware that we have the best mechanics at our dealership and it's clear to me how much you all enjoy working on cars and doing the job right. Even though this is a tough situation for you all, I am totally confident that you'll get through this without the dealership losing any of it's reputation that you all have created here."

"When Pete's wife passed away last year, our business

department really struggled. Everyone loved Sue and it was a huge loss for us. What I learned from that experience is that we are all family here. When we have a tragedy like this, we all have to deal with it in our own way, but we also have to deal with it together. It's finding that balance that is important. We must respect each other as individuals who deal with tragedy in their own way, but also respect that we are all part of this dealership and we all depend on each other to be successful at what we do. "

"When I was playing baseball, we lost a coach who was everything to me. I actually signed with the Angels, not because they offered me more money, but because I would be spending my Summer with Joe as my coach, and that was more important to me. My agent was a little pissed, but he got over it. Anyway, when Joe died, I was crushed. I wanted to just close down and go away, but I learned pretty quickly how important it is not to close down. I know you are feeling the same now. You want to close down your heart and get away from the pain. I promise you though, the key is not to close down your heart, but to open your hearts. I know that once we started talking about Joe and sharing the stories we had, we became better players. By talking about Joe and sharing experiences, we started to laugh again. The heavy weight of sadness no longer dragged us down because we wanted to play better and honor the memory of our friend whom we loved so much."

"That is the key, I think. That's what got me through the loss of Joe. That's what got Pete through the loss of Sue. And that's what will get you through the loss of Jack. Open your hearts and share the great stories created because you were lucky enough to have known Jack. We can't bring him back, and that truly is sad, but we can keep his memory alive by opening our hearts."

Mr. Jones pauses to let this all sink in before he sits back in his seat and signals the servers for another round of drinks.

"So I'm in no hurry today. How about you all sharing some stories about Jack? I hear he was quite the jokester in the pit."

There is a hesitant quiet in the room until finally JC starts out. "Remember the time …. "

For a better part of the afternoon, the pit crew and Mr. Jones stayed in the break room and told wonderful stories of Jack. There was plenty of laughter to go with the tears, as everyone opened up and shared their experiences about Jack. Other employees walked by the windows of the break room and obviously had no clue what was going on in there.

Johnny sat back and took it all in. What a wonderful owner this man was. Mechanics at a car dealership are not the face of the company. They are the ones who quietly sit in the back of the room at the company Christmas party and leave as soon as it's possible to do so without getting into trouble. Yet here they are sitting in the break room with the owner sharing wonderful stories, laughing and crying together.

Mr. Jones knew when it was time to conclude this meeting and stands up one final time.

"I really appreciate you all sharing your stories of Jack with me. It helps me to understand the pain you are going through and it firms up my commitment to helping his family out too. I'll tell Pete in front of all you that I have no problem with you all taking the rest of the day off. Make sure the cars are okay for the night and go home. You'll be paid for a regular days work and tomorrow you can get back to taking care of our customers. Pete and I will let you know when the service will be and it goes without saying, we'll close down the pit that day with pay. I truly am sorry for your loss and appreciate each one of you being a part of our family here."

With that, they all get up to head back to the pit. Not surprisingly, none of them seem too anxious to leave. Pete reminds them that they are welcome to leave, but each one dismisses the thought and continues on with their work.

Within a half hour, the pit is back to full throttle with everyone working together as before to get the cars out of the shop.

Mr. Jones comes in and finds Pete at the counter going over some paper work. "You did tell them they could go home, right? Why are they still here?"

Pete looks up at Mr. Jones and smiles, "They're mechanics …. This is home."

As the afternoon approaches closing time, they are all busy putting the final touches on what has been a very emotional, exhausting day here in the pit. Johnny thinks about the day as he walks to his car and is completely impressed on how the events of the day played out. What a great group of people.

As he open the door to his car and climbs in, he is suddenly sitting in George's office looking at George who is smiling.

21

———

The Reunion

"Welcome back, Johnny! Nice work."

Johnny is stunned as he looks around, then back at George, "Nice work? I didn't do anything."

"Well you didn't do much for Pete I suppose, but you did plant some nice seeds in the pit and you did make some customers happy with their cars, and that's always a good thing. Especially for a guy who use to work on cars by putting air in his tires, right?" George smiles at Johnny who is unamused.

"Did Mary do this? I know my thoughts about God making Jack die so I'd have something to talk about was kinda lame, but she didn't have to just throw me out like that."

"Oh Johnny, you give angels way too much credit. I'm the only one who can pull people out of an assignment. They didn't need you anymore and I decided to bring you back to move on." George says with a smile.

"But I didn't do anything. I didn't have one meaningful conversation with Pete while I was there. Did I miss something here?" Johnny asks in a complete state of confusion.

"You didn't miss a thing, Johnny. You have to remember that this is a free will planet, so when we develop an assignment for you, we have no idea what direction the assignment might go. When you take an assignment, you are merely there in case the assignment goes south and you need to get involved. Some times an assignment goes much better than we anticipated and our recruit turns out to not be needed. That's great news for us. It's not wasted time at all. We were prepared for the worst and are happy when the assignment goes so well that our recruits are not actually utilized. It's a good thing, Johnny."

"So Pete figured it all out on his own?" Johnny asks.

"No. Remember when you and the angels were talking about his support team? How the angels were concerned about Sues family and how they could easily make Pete's life miserable if he starts to fade? Turns out Sue's family is a huge bonus for Pete and have really stepped up in helping Pete out. Stephanie canceled a trip to Europe and spent some time at Pete's, teaching him a lot about cooking. – turns out Pete has learned to love cooking and is getting quite good at it – and talking to her nieces about their Mom. As for her parents, we were worried that their strong personalities could really put a lot of stress on Pete, but it turns out both the mother and father stepped up and really helped Pete out. Her mother calls often and comes down from Chicago to help him out once a month, while her dad has helped Pete out a lot with all the legal stuff that people have to deal with when someone dies. So it turns out that with Sue's family, Mr. Jones and all the people at the dealership, Pete has a great support system around him and there really is no need for you any more."

Johnny sits back and considers all that George has said. "Wow, that really is good news for Pete. He really is a good man and now that you've told me, it makes sense. I was getting frustrated because Pete was giving me zero opportunities to talk with him. He never showed any stress or frustration and I was getting concerned that he was burying his emotions in a macho, must be strong manner, when the truth was he actually was doing very well and just didn't have that much stress. That's nice."

George smiles and relaxes as he sees that Johnny is beginning to understand.

"So what happens to me?" asks Johnny.

George casually responds, "Well you and I can discuss another assignment if you want, or you're welcome to start your eternity."

Johnny interrupts, "Not me here, I meant me there. Are those people walking into another day hearing about my death now? I think that would be more than enough suffering for those great people, don't you?"

George smiles, "Oh no, we wouldn't put that on those people. Joe's taking over your spot there."

Johnny quickly jumps in, "God is taking my spot?"

"Oh yea, he jumped at the chance. God loves working on mechanical things and has always been fascinated by engines. He didn't hesitate to take this assignment. He's going to be you for about a year or so Earth time and then retire. He's really excited for the opportunity to work on cars for a bit." George says.

Johnny seems a little uncomfortable at the thought of God being in his body.

"So you're saying that right now, God is inside my body working on Mrs. Adams distributor?"

"Sure is, and having a ball doing so. Just think, Johnny, you're going to have a 100% success rate as long as God is working in your body. Why, Pete's going to think you're a genius. In fact it wouldn't surprise me at all if God takes this assignment two or three years down the road. He's going to make you look good, Johnny. God doesn't make any mistakes, ya know." George says with a hint of joy.

Johnny sits back to consider all this. He's not sure how he feels about it, but he does at least take comfort in knowing his friends back in the pit will be taken care of.

"Does he do this all the time?" Johnny asks.

"Well I wouldn't say all the time, but he is the ultimate creator. He loves to visit the planets he's created and get involved with them at their level. He has created so many wonderful worlds and has often told me, ' What's the point of creating all these worlds if I can't go and enjoy them?' I tell you, Johnny, this is one God that really knows how to enjoy eternity."

Johnny smiles as he thinks about it, "It's funny how we all think of God as being this big, powerful, intimidating figure when we are living. Then we die and come to this side only to find out he's just a regular Joe."

George laughs, "Well I wouldn't call him a regular Joe, Johnny, but you are right. God is baffled at how you humans start out okay saying God is love and God's love is unconditional, but then you spend all your time and energy creating religions and rules that make God extremely conditional. He's told me to send someone down there to explain what unconditional love is all the time and the truth is I have – several times – and you humans crucify them, assassinate them or write them off as some kind of lunatic. It's a crazy world you humans have created for yourselves, but God continues to love you and enjoys those opportunities when he can spend some time down there."

Johnny nods in agreement as he smiles. "So it looks like Pete is going to be alright, what do you have for me now?"

George smiles at Johnny, "You've been a big help to us here at the GETA Foundation, so I wouldn't have a problem in letting you get started on your own eternity. Or if you want another assignment, I certainly have a couple you could look at. Your call."

Johnny sits back in thought. This is not an easy decision. On the one hand, he's getting the hang of how the assignments work and thinks it would be good to continue on with another assignment. On the other hand he has no idea what his eternity is, but he has a feeling that it might be a good idea not to put it off any longer than he has to.

"It's not an easy decision, being that I have no idea what my eternity is all about, you know." he says to George.

George smiles, "Indeed. And if I told you what your eternity was all about, there wouldn't be a decision to be made."

"Can I have some time to think about it?" Johnny asks.

"Absolutely." says George.

At that moment, the door behind Johnny opens and a very young version of Johnny's wife, Beth, walks in.

Johnny turns and falls out of his seat. "BETH!?!"

She smiles at Johnny with the most radiant smile as Johnny lays on the floor in absolute shock. Beth looks great. So beautiful and bursting with love.

Johnny turns and looks to George who is smiling.

"I thought I'd bring her in to help you decide what you want to do." George says

Johnny gets up and goes to Beth and embraces her in a hug that would likely break some ribs if she had any. George looks on with admiration, knowing that this man has been away from the love of his life for a long time and he is in no hurry to rush the moment.

After an affectionate time of embracing, Beth surfaces and looks deep into Johnny's overflowing eyes, "I know a place we could go have a drink and talk about it." she says as she holds this man whom she missed for so long. She looks over to George who simply winks at her.

As the two step out the door, George takes a deep breath of relief at the outcome, sits back and kicks his feet up on his desk and puts his hands behind his head in a posture of satisfaction.

"Now that's how you work enough!"

22

The Judgement

As Beth and Johnny step out the GETA Foundation door, Johnny realizes that they have just stepped into his old neighborhood Pub that he hung out at for so long.

Beth is quick to lay down the rules. "Keep in mind that a lot has changed since you were last here, Johnny. And also keep in mind that an attractive young woman like me would never go out to dinner with an old man like you, so try not to sound old and say something stupid."

Johnny looks at her and she winks with that engaging smile. Then he looks down at his hands and realizes they are without wrinkles. He turns to the mirrored beer advertisement hanging on the wall and sees a much younger version of himself standing next to the most beautiful woman he has ever known.

As they make their way to table 2, Johnny remembers the night Kim's Dad, Jack, came to show her the nursing scores. As they settle into their seats, Johnny looks around.

He doesn't notice any of the faces from the past, but he does notice that his Santa's hat is on the wall above the servers station. He also looks at his seat with the Tom Collins sitting to the side and is flooded with the memories of a time long ago.

A server comes to greet them. "How are you folks tonight? My name is Bobbi and I'll be your server tonight. Can I get you something to drink?"

Beth orders a glass of wine and Johnny the usual Tom Collins.

"Good choice, sir. We have a special tonight on our Tom Collins. Half price and all the proceeds from them goes to the Johnny Foundation."

Johnny perks up, "The what foundation?"

"The Johnny Foundation. You folks aren't from around here, I'm guessing?"

Beth is quick to answer for them both, "No, we're just passing through, but do tell us about the foundation."

Bobbi is happy to continue, "It's a foundation we started here at the bar named after a regular who passed away a few years back. His name was Johnny and every Christmas, he played Santa Clause for the underprivileged children out on the east side of town. When he passed away, his daughter donated all the money from his estate she inherited and gave it to this Pub to keep Johnny's work with the children going. It's become quite a foundation for the kids and their families."

"Well that sounds like a great program. Why don't you bring me a Tom Collins as well." says Beth

"Great!" says Bobbi as she heads back to the servers station to get her order.

Beth turns to Johnny, "That sounds like Elizabeth doesn't it? I imagine after she sold the house and whatever she could inside, and with your frugal spending, I'm sure there was a pretty good amount in the bank, she probably gave them a pretty good nest egg to start their foundation, don't you think?"

Johnny smiles, "I suppose your right, Beth. We raised her right. She always seemed to have enough and never wanted more."

He pauses as he takes in Beths beauty. "God, I've missed you."

Beth reaches over and takes his hand and smiles, "I think I came close to being thrown out of Heaven because I was bugging my angel so much to get you on this side. I swear, that angel sure earned her wings with me annoying her like I did."

They just look at each other as the drinks are delivered.

"Can I get you something to eat?" Bobbi asks.

Johnny looks at Beth then Bobbi, "You know I came here a few years back during a business trip and I remember having a Fried Chicken dinner here that was just excellent..."

Bobbi confirms, "Oh yes sir, it's still our best seller."

"Excellent!' says Johnny, "I'll take it. I also remember the bartender was a girl named Sue."

Bobbi jumps in again, "Yes sir, she owns the bar now."

"Really?" says Johnny, "Good for her! She seemed like a girl who was going places."

"Yea, when the previous owner was slowing down, he made sure that when he died, Sue would become the legal owner. He passed away last October and everything was turned over to Sue. Couldn't happen to a nicer person if you ask me."

"Well she seemed like a good one." Johnny agrees.

"And for you mam?" Bobbi turns to Beth.

Beth smiles at Johnny, then turns to Bobbi, "Well if he says your Fried Chicken is that good, I'll go with that."

"Excellent. I'll get that order up right away. Do you want any appetizers while you wait?" Bobbi asks.

"No thanks, we'll just have the chicken dinners." says Beth.

As Bobbi heads to put in their order, Beth turns to Johnny who has a surprised look on his face.

"Don't look at me that way, young man, they don't have any scales on this side, you know. It doesn't matter what you eat. I can have Fried Chicken or anything else now!" Beth says with a deep tone of gratitude.

Johnny laughs as he takes a sip from his drink, "I guess I have a lot to learn on this side." he pauses in thought before he continues, "You know, I really enjoyed the work I did for the GETA Foundation, and I think I was doing pretty good. I wonder if George would be too disappointed if I don't go back there?"

Beth laughs out loud as Johnny almost takes offense to her being humored by his comments. "Oh Johnny, you do have a lot to learn. There's a reason why God put George in charge of Earth operations. He is an expert at making people think they have a choice, when in reality they don't." she pauses as Johnny looks confused.

"Johnny, everybody does two assignments with George before they can move on to their eternity. He just makes you believe that it's your choice. God knew what he was doing when he put George in charge, that's for sure."

Johnny takes a sip from his drink as he considers what Beth is saying. "Well I'll be. Everyone does them, huh? What is the point of everyone doing two assignments?"

"God feels that there are so many different perceptions on Earth about God, Heaven, Hell and all that, it's good to have a transition period. He calls it time to shake out the cobwebs of earthly perceptions and prepare them for the awesome reality of their eternity. After a couple assignments with George, most people are understanding that many of the teachings about God really aren't that close to reality. George is very good about creating two assignments to help each individual get a feel for their eternity."

Beth takes a break as Bobbi comes back with their Fried Chicken. "Can I get you anything else? How about another drink?" asks Bobbi.

"That's a splendid idea Bobbi. Another round would be great." Johnny says.

As Bobbi heads back to the station, Johnny looks to Beth and smiles, "I suppose it doesn't matter how many drinks we have on this side too, right?" he says with a devilish smile.

Beth shakes her head, "Oh Johnny, if we sat here and had drinks until they closed, it wouldn't affect us at all, that's true. But it sure would make these people wonder what we're made of, so behave yourself!"

Johnny gets a good laugh as he takes a big bite from his chicken.

"So the two assignments I had were specifically designed for me?" he asks.

Beth puts down her chicken to respond. "Well the assignments were real situations on Earth to be sure, but George gave them to you specifically because they were best suited to your transition to this side."

Johnny thinks about it, "How so?"

"Well your first assignment with Sarah was a validation assignment. Everybody has a gift and yours was the beautiful message you gave the children and the people here at the Pub that if you ask for more, you'll never have enough, but if you ask for enough, you'll never need more. It's a beautiful message Johnny, and you did a wonderful job of promoting it to those who needed it. So your first assignment was to show you how your heart served you well in your life."

Beth pauses to let that sink in, and to grab another bite of that delicious chicken. Johnny is considering what she is saying.

"Your second assignment was what I call your dessert of humble pie. Pete was able to recover from a very tragic loss because he was surrounded by so much love from the many people in his life, and you had nothing to do with it. You just fixed cars, and that was the point. It's not you that makes the changes, it's the love. Instead of getting frustrated at having no opportunities to talk with Pete, you should celebrate the fact that you didn't need to. There was enough love in the hearts of those around him to keep him strong and that's what we celebrate."

Johnny sits back and takes another draw from his drink as he considers all that Beth is telling him.

"It's almost like the judgement day that everyone talks about on the other side." He says with a smile.

Beth agrees, "Exactly. The people on the other side have the right ideas, but unfortunately, their perception is compromised by worldly rules and mechanical teachings of earthly religions. They think a judgement day is a courtroom scene with God on a high pedestal looking down at you sternly as you try to justify your existence. That's not God. God is love and his love is unconditional. The assignments help us to understand the gifts we were given and that we are Gods instruments of love and we should celebrate the advancement of love regardless of what our role is in doing so. That's the transition that is needed as we move on to our eternity."

Johnny is relaxed and at peace with all that Beth has said, as Bobbi comes by to see if they want anything else.

As Johnny looks around the Pub, he asks Bobbi about the Santa hat on the wall.

"That was the hat that this Johnny guy wore. Sue put a bell on it and every time a server gets enough on a tip, she rings the bell. Apparently this Johnny was very big on telling kids not to ask for more, but to ask for enough, so Sue wants us to remember that."

Johnny smiles at Beth, then asks the server about sign above the hat.

"The heart of flames with the 142 in it?"

"Yes, that's an interesting picture. Must have a story behind it?" Johnny asks, knowing full well what it is.

"Sue put that up there. She says it's to remind us that it only takes one simple act of kindness to be the spark that ignites the entire community. Nobody knows what the 142 is for, and Sue won't tell anyone, but it's a nice thought."

"A nice thought indeed." Johnny says as he and Beth get up to leave and Bobbi heads to the servers station to pick up some more drinks for table 6.

"So are you ready for your eternity, Johnny?" Beth asks.

Before he can answer, they hear the chime of the Santa hat being rung and look over to see Bobbi looking at them with a big smile.

Johnny turns back to Beth. "It looks like we've done enough here. Time to move on." he says.

As they walk out the door, they find themselves in what seems to be a very large, empty room. In the distance is what appears to be an angel walking towards them. Beth turns to Johnny and pats him on the back.

"Well time for me to head out Johnny boy. Ya done good. Have a nice eternity."

Johnny turns to Beth, "Wait a minute, where are you going?"

Beth smiles at him, "I have cars to work on Johnny, and they only give me an hour for lunch, ya know. That chicken was a good choice. See ya later Johnny."

With that, Beth – or Joe – or God – smiles and disappears just like that.

Johnny stands there speechless as the angel draws near.

"Welcome, Johnny. I'm your guardian angel. I don't have a name unless you want to give me one. I'm connected to your heart though, so you'll never have to call for me."

Johnny looks at the angel, then back to where Beth was just standing… then back to the angel, who smiles.

"Follow me and I'll show you where she really is."

With that, Johnny follows the angel to begin his eternity.

The End

I'VE SAID ENOUGH!

www.ingramcontent.com/pod-product-compliance
Lightning Source LLC
Chambersburg PA
CBHW021151110726
47900CB00002B/523